QUEEN OF KINGS

A WORLD OF ZAVINIA PREQUEL

C.M HANO

Copyright © 2021 by C.M. Hano
C. M. Hano Books
All rights reserved.
Kingsland, GA USA
cmhanoauthor.org

Paperback ISBN: 9798985389036
Character Art Paperback ISBN: 9798403252683

This is a work of fiction, Names, characters, places, and incidents either are the product of the author's imagination or are used factiously. Any resemblance to actual persons, living or dead, events, or locales is entirely coincidental.

All rights reserved. No part of this book may be reproduced in any manner whatsoever without written permission except in the case of brief quotations embodied in critical articles and reviews. First Printing, 2022

Formatting By: Charlotte Brassington & Sue Allerton
Proofreader: Charlotte Brassington
Campus Map Created By: The Illustrated Page Book Design
Cover Design Created By: The Illustrated Page Book Design
Map Created By: V. M. Jaskerina
Cover Art By: Tóth Júlia (julia.toth227@gmail.com)

FOREWORD

Please note that this story is not suitable for persons under the age of eighteen.

WARNING: This book contains sexually explicit scenes, adult language, and violence. It may be considered offensive or disturbing to some readers. It is intended for sale to adults ONLY, as defined by the laws of the country in which you made your purchase.

PLAYLIST

Heart Attack - Demi Lovato

Fascination - Tuxedo Junction Band

Intentions - Justin Bieber

Shivers - Ed Sheeran

Sex With Me - Rihanna

I Knew You Were Trouble - Taylor Swift

Warrior - Demi Lovato

Hands To Myself - Selena Gomez

Traitor - Olivia Rodrigo

Love The Way You Lie - Eminem (FT. Rihanna)

Before You Go - Lewis Capaldi

This Means War - Avenge Sevenfold

Skyscraper - Demi Lovato

Vulnerable - Selena Gomez

Stay With Me - Sam Smith

Monster - Skillet

Love Is Gone - Dylan Mathew

This One is for all my Smut lovers!

CHOOSE YOUR ELEMENT

CHOOSE YOUR ORDER

 ROGUE

 HUNTER

 WARRIOR

 MAGE

KLESTRIA ACADEMY

DEFINITION GUIDE

High King - Ruler of Zavinia
King - Ruler of Individual country within Zavinia
Queen - Ruler of a country alongside a King
Rogue - Silent Assassin
Mage - Conjurer of magic
Warrior - Super soldier
Hunter - Master of animals
Druid - Conjurer of magic, Master of Animals, superior to all other Orders.
Elemental - the ability to control one of the four elements. (water, fire, earth, air)
Elite Elemental - the ability to control all four elements.

Prologue

XANDER

We got the notice just this morning. A queen in need of a king. There is to be a grand ball held at the Cathedral within Klestria. I crumple the parchment in my fists while sitting on my throne.

"I take it you have heard?" Jett Covaxs, the air rogue from Davianiansphere, stands across from me with his hand on the hilt of his sheathed sword, a smug smirk forming on his very punchable face.

"Is this a joke?" I ask him.

"No, I don't think Sarrs would joke about something like this."

"Who is she?"

"Don't know and do not care. I'm not the one marrying her." I growl at the very thought. The only reason I am going is to prevent Sarrs from coming here and causing problems for disobeying a direct order.

"Kai will make an honorable match." I comment and Jett seems surprised by it.

"Who knew you had a soft side?" He mocks.

"This may pose a problem." I state.

"And what problem is that?" Kai's voice interrupts as he walks through my throne hall doors.

"Where are my fucking guards?!" I growl getting to my feet.

"Oh, I thought we were having a little pow wow here. Enzo is right behind me." At the mention of the fire king's name, he saunters inside.

"What the fuck are we going to do about this?" He yells, seeming to match my own concerns.

"Nothing. What can we do? She is not a threat. I heard she has no magic." Kai states.

"Look at you, already sticking up for your wife and you haven't stuck your cock in her tight pussy yet." Jett remarks.

"Watch your mouth. She is a queen." Kai snarls.

"None of you will do anything but protect her and bring her directly to me." Another deeper, older, and darker voice chimes in causing shivers to run down my spine.

The scent of cinnamon and blood flood my throne hall as *he* steps out of the shadows.

Instantly, all four of us drop to kneel before our true king.

"Rialynne Faith is to be protected at all costs."

"Yes, Sire. But who is she?" I ask as we get to our feet.

As he stepped into the light, his flame-colored hair gleamed, highlighting his bright green eyes that failed to distract from the horrific scar he got from a gash by a rogue assassin. A constant reminder of the day his wife died.

"What? Who is she?" Kai gasps. Before King Sarr's rule, King Roderick and his wife ruled over Zavinia. He went into hiding after that day when it was discovered that Sarrs hired the assassin.

"My daughter."

"Why didn't you mention this before?" I ask him.

"Because I thought she was dead." He states, sounding pained with the news.

"You must understand that day was a blur of chaos. Ria, my sweet Ria, was attacked, and she was bleeding from her head right next to her mother. I thought I lost both. Your father," he points to me, "saved me and delivered the news all at once."

"I'm sorry." Kai says.

"Don't be. It brings all the plans forward." He is talking about the plans for him to take back Zavinia from Sarrs.

"How? She has been the ward of Sarrs all these years. He has been her father figure. Anything we tell her; she wouldn't believe it." I told him.

"No matter. There will be an attack the night of the engagement ball. Be prepared to take her under the guise of saving her and bring her to me. She will understand it all." He states.

"You are planning to attack innocents?" I question, the only one of us that is willing to challenge his morals.

"You think those nobles are innocent?" he growls. "I have given my orders, if you wish to challenge me then do so, otherwise shut your trap and follow through."

"Yes, sire." I say with a bow.

"Good. Do not let me down. Or else your pretty heads will no longer be attached to your shoulders. There is nothing more precious to me than my daughter."

Chapter One

RIALYNNE

"They say the four kings are good men. Powerful in their elements. Righteous too." I looked up from the book I was reading, to the three women sitting in their wingback chairs across the mahogany tea table. The same spot we always sit each time we come into the common room for quiet time. Not that it was ever quiet in here with these three always rambling. Normally, I did not get frustrated with the gossip, I have gotten good at tuning them out, but today, I couldn't control it.

There was always resistance when I tried to manipulate the thing inside of me, always a fight with it, although its prongs were burrowed into my skull. It was forbidden to touch it. To speak of the curse that was bestowed upon me. And most of all, I was forbidden to touch the device that aided in breaking it. Not that it truly broke the curse, more like simmered it down.

Not that these ladies would know if I did anything to it. Which did not surprise me at all considering their choice in occupation. They were Ladies of the Cathedral of Ares; the large ivory tower was constructed with the brick and mortar from the dunes of the Klestrian Desert. Ever since the goddess left the earth to take her place amongst the stars, cathedrals were placed throughout all territories within Zavinia to worship and praise her. Even the smaller villages within each sphere had them. The Ladies of the Cathedral spent their lives as pure liaisons that helped spread the ancient text everywhere through teachings. They took in orphans that needed a safe spot to stay until they grew to the age of being an adult.

Today, they were extra talkative, but also, they dressed in their formal wear. Adorned in ivory dresses and bonnets, they seemed to be on edge, anxious even. I knew that today they would be extremely mindful of the way they walked, sat, and talked. With the royal procession making their appearance tonight, everyone was on their best behavior. Everyone, except for me. Hidden beneath all the cosmetics and layers of silk fabrics of the gown, the screaming voice of a woman trying to escape echoed in my head.

The voice that was silenced when I was six years old by one assassination attempt that killed my family and scarred me for life, heightened by the golden headband atop my head just above my pointed ears. A hearing aid with sides decorated in golden leaves, to hide the prongs that are embedded in my bones- and the very center front is a single diamond, showing my status as a royal. Not that I cared for titles. All the money and power in the world would never be able to bring back my hearing. No, just a device to help aid it.

"Righteous?" Lady Periwinkle asked mid-stitch. She was a younger human, around twenty-six years old, two years younger than my twenty-eight. Not that, years mattered to blood elfs like it did to humans. Her bright green eyes reminded me of the giant oak trees in the Magianinasphere. I could not see any other features besides the exposed fair color upon her face and hands. "They aren't righteous. The four kings of Zavinia are tyrants that cast out anyone that is not their Order or Element. Ares should rain down upon them, just to teach them some humility."

My stomach rolls. Four kings, each ruling one of the surrounding land masses. King Enzo Covaxs rules the frost covered lands of the Avaniansphere opposite his cousin King Jett Covaxs who rules the southern territory of the Davianiansphere. Both bring in timber and furs each season that are used for construction of new buildings or weapons. Not that I am privy to such knowledge.

"Hogwash, those kings are no more brutal than King Sarrs himself." I didn't even try to hide my eye roll at Lady Willow's praise for the high king of Zavinia.

King Sarrs is a blood elf with gold for hair and eyes of red. A fire elemental gifted with the strength and bloodlust of ten thousand. I should be grateful for him. He was the one who saved me the day my family was bleeding and dying on the throne hall floors of the Emerald Palace. The building was crafted of millions of green gems that match the eye color that has been passed down to every Klestrian Royal to include its queen.

It was destroyed that same day. Good riddance.

"Rialynne, that is not how a queen sits." Lady Stephanie scolds me. Making the other two stop bickering to examine the lackadaisical way I am slouched in my chair.

"Shoulders back."

"Legs crossed."

"Chin up." All three of them corrected something. Getting to my feet, I gently close my book, walk over to the vast bookshelf that is mounted to the back wall, and push it back into place. It was a dry part of the story anyway.

"Ladies," I give them a nod, turning on my heel, praying they would not stop me from fleeing. But no such luck, I did not make it out in time.

"Where do you think you are going?" Lady Willow asks from behind.

"I need to get ready for the ball." I answered her.

"Oh, we will assist you." Turning, I immediately produce an excuse for them to stay put.

"No. That really isn't necessary. A queen should be able to dress herself and besides, I am twenty-eight. Plenty old enough to doll myself up for a dance." I tell them before turning and grabbing the handle.

"It isn't just a dance, child." Lady Willow states. I try to contain my frustrated grunt but fail, miserably. "This royal ball is meant for you to be chosen by one of the kings. Or for King Sarrs to announce his choice."

My stomach clenches again. Not at the mention of this ridiculous ball, but because of the arranged marriage that I will have no choice or say in. A queen should be able to choose her husband. A woman should be able to. It was this way during the old world. But ever since Ares left, women have been forced into submission by men and I've about had it up to here with these misogynistic laws. When King Sarrs finally dies, I will inherit the realm and with my power, women will rise. And the men of this world will rue the day they thought they could control us.

"Of course." I state and they all follow me out of the common room, down the hall towards the right and straight through the crimson painted doors leading into my room. My stomach started to clench as they began their discussion of the potential marriage. I know I need to get away from them before I lose control. "I need to relieve myself; I will be out in a moment."

Without waiting for a response from them, I rush over to my bathroom, close the door and hurl into the toilet.

Goddess be damned.

Getting to my feet, I move to the sink after flushing the fluids down the pipes, turning the faucet, cupping the cool liquid in my hands and bringing it to my mouth to sip, soothing the acid burning my throat. I swirl the liquid in my mouth to get rid of the taste of vomit.

"You are not a queen. This," I say while I reach up and touch the cool metal atop my head. "does not make you one. Goddess why? Why me?" tears drip down my cheeks before a knock sounds and I turn towards the door. "Just a minute."

"Rialynne, we do not have another minute." Lady Willow states. Right because having the title of queen means no fucking privacy. Wiping the misguided tears from my face, I rinse my mouth out with some mint-paste before turning and heading back into my room.

I cringe at the crimson gown that is draped across the ivory sheets of my four-poster bed. Stepping up to the floor-length mirror to the right of my closet door. Boney cold fingers brush against my skin as the laces of the ivory corset I was wearing is undone and pulled from my body.

When I am down to my silk slip, I look at myself in the mirror and admire the crimson color of my hair. The texture and color are the only physical features I inherited from my mother. Even with all the conditioners known to Zavinia, nothing can tame the way it flickers on its own like a fire.

"Oh, Rialynne, you look absolutely regal." Lady Periwinkle exclaims as soon as the silky material is conformed to my body. A white sash is wrapped around my waist to balance the color, with two golden chains connecting to the ivory leggings I am wearing underneath the skirts. The straps are beautiful and hang off my shoulders ever-so slightly with a nice golden trim flowing down the back. My ears are pierced with golden hoops to match the golden chain around my neck, which holds a single diamond at the center making it match my tiara. A breast plate is attached to the front in case there are rogue assassins at the ball.

A distant memory flashes, old but not any less painful.

The one good thing to come out of me being a queen, is that I can choose my own footwear. I always choose to wear knee-high leather boots. A color to match anything I am wearing and reliable shoes if I need to run or fight. "Alright, no more ogling at her. It is time to present her to the procession. Are you ready, my dear?"

Looking at Lady Willow, I give her a brief smile before reaching out and hugging her. I do the same with Lady Stephanie and Lady Periwinkle, because these three ladies have been with me for my entire time here.

"Dry your tears. It's time." Lady Willow said, wiping at her own.

QUEEN OF KINGS

The ball room is luxurious with marbled floors that glisten off the lights from the chandeliers floating above us. Nobles from all five territories are in attendance and as I make my way onto the cerulean rug that flows down the middle, everything stops. The noise of chatter, the music of the band, and even my breathing.

Keep it together.

"Presenting, her royal highness, Queen Rialynne Faith." The door man, who I think is named Andras, proclaims. My hands are pressed together in front of my navel as I walk to the front of the room. I discreetly dig my nails into my skin to prevent me from fidgeting, but I do not think it is working. Once I am at the front of the room, I stop in the middle and bow to the five males seated at the front.

King Sarrs stands to his feet, the four others follow suit, and then I wait with my heart thrashing in my chest with anticipation.

"Welcome to Klestria. Tonight, you will witness the union of our next queen and king. A union that is blessed by Ares herself. Rialynne," he says, and I look up at him. "Come and meet your new fiancé."

Please do not be ugly. Please do not be ugly.

My feet move forward, and I stop right in front of Sarrs, waiting for one of the kings to step forward, but when none do, I begin to panic. My eyes frantically drift from one face to the next, none of these bastards are showing a single hint of emotion.

I see movement out of the corner of my eye, a flash of black, and then the scent of seafoam washes over me. "My queen."

Turning, I catch onto the male standing in front of me. King Kai Pace from the Oceaniansphere.

"A human?" I whisper with surprise. He tilts his head sideways and assesses me from head to toe. I return the favor, starting from the thick waves of blonde and brown atop his head, to the roundness of his human ears. Along the hair that covers the squareness of his jawline and over the plump nature of his lips.

His body is clearly well-crafted underneath the fine materials of his black tunic and pants. Two daggers are sheathed at each hip. A rogue by the looks of his appearance. When my eyes move back to meet him, I get temporarily lost in the depths of the two pools that seem to be pulling me in.

"A rogue? A human?" I mutter and he nods.

"Let's clear the floor so the couple can take their first dance." I gulp hard when he reaches out for me to take his arm. I do not notice that I am moving until his hand is on my hip and the other one is interlocked with mine. Our bodies barely have a breath of air between them causing many different sensations to explode all over my body.

"A human. A rogue." I repeat.

"A blood elf." I snap my gaze to him. "I thought we were simply stating the obvious?"

"I'm sorry, I didn't mean to offend you. I'm just surprised."

"As am I." he states with a smirk. We move in-sync, gliding across the marble stones to the soft tempo of the violin. My blood pounds through my ears, almost drowning out the beautiful orchestra. "You should calm down."

"What?" I say looking at him. He catches me with his gaze again. A heat rises in my cheeks and if I were not wearing blush, I am sure he would notice.

"If they see you are afraid, then it will not leave a good impression."

"I'm not afraid." I snap. I feel his hand slide from my hip to my back, pressing me closer to him. The heat of his body overwhelmed mine, making my core tighten with a new feeling.

"Then why is your heart thundering so hard?" he asks then twirls me without warning. Drawing me back into him, our hips touch as our hands interlace both above our heads and at the waist.

"It isn't." He scoffs at my response. Twirling me again and then catching my back, dipping me before pulling me back up. A brief light-headedness comes over me with the swift movement. The music dies down and we turn and face King Sarrs.

"King Kai, Queen Rialynne, tomorrow your union will be solidified in the Cathedral of Ares. May the goddess bless you with many heirs." King Sarrs states and the crowd cheers. Kai squeezes my hand, but I do not squeeze it back. I want to pry my hand from his just as quickly as he took it. "Dance and feast."

I needed to get out of here. Away from the bodies, the heat, the music. Everything and everyone. Wrenching my hand free, I give Kai a quick bow before I excuse myself.

Rushing out the ball room, I quickly walk towards the direction of the gardens. It is in the opposite direction of my room. Once I am outside, I suck in the brisk night air, and take a moment to walk towards the gazebo.

"Rialynne."

Chapter Two

JETT

As we line up at the front of the hall, I try not to scowl at all the gossiping nobles. We have waited and prepared for this night. The plan is set and will start as soon as this so-called queen makes her appearance. I pity Kai, he will have to dance with her. We made the decision as one that Kai should be the one to pretend to be engaged to her.

Marriage is not something I would ever want to endure in my entire life. It sounds dreadful and I like to have my fill of pussy when the time calls. Many of my whores are more than willing to do what I like without complaint.

Being a king has its advantages.

A familiar scent washes over me, reminding me of home. A mix of all four elements. I sniff the air and notice the other three doing the same. Trying to pinpoint the potent scent. The doors open and in comes the most beautiful woman I have ever seen in my entire life. Something deep inside my soul rises within me. Stonger than anything I've felt before. My inner alpha rising to claim his mate.

Mine.

I growl and I can't help but notice the entire room fades as she glides down the aisle. A picture of perfection adorned in crimson and gold. The beautiful way her hair flickers into the air, reminds me of a light guiding lost souls in the night. That is what she will be for me. A light that will guide me from the darkest parts of myself. Red suits her. Compliments the beautiful olive color of her skin and bright green of her eyes.

I will have you as mine, Red.

A growl escapes me when I see Kai step up to claim her. It's low and occurs as Sarrs is discussing their first dance. Having to watch him take her, seeing she is uncomfortable, has my fingers itching to rip him from her arms. I need to get out of here before I do something stupid. As the music dies down, I see a distant look glinting in her eyes.

I watch her intently, noticing the way the pulse in her neck thunders with the anxiety I am sure she is feeling.

I can't hide the smirk forming on my mouth as I watch her make a break for it. I see Xander signal for me to come over with them. No doubt to discuss the woman who my soul is now aching for. I won't tell them. But I will not allow anyone to prevent me from getting what is rightfully mine.

Chapter Three

ENZO

*M*ine.

Fire red hair and eyes that shine as bright as green gems, this blood elf is the most gorgeous sight I have ever seen before. If I did not have to stand here and watch Kai sweep her off her feet, I would take his place in a heartbeat.

Something inside me called out to her the moment she stepped through those doors. It intensified the moment her scent washed over me. I suspect the other kings have had the same reaction; they all seem to flock to her. Kai cannot seem to keep his eyes off her.

"We all need to talk." Xander whispers in my ear as Rialynne makes a beeline for the back door. With Sarrs busy, we huddle around each other.

"Did you all feel that?" Kai asks.

"Yes." The three of us say at the same time.

"This could be a problem." Xander mumbles.

"Why?" Jett asks.

"Because you idiot, our inner alphas have claimed her. We cannot have her, not really." Xander says.

"You sound almost disappointed." I tease him.

"No. The reality of this is, she is just a woman, and we have our orders. When the attack starts, take her, and get the hell out of here. Then we can wash our hands of her." Xander states.

"I don't think I can." Jett admits. "I mean have you seen her?"

"Have you held her?" Kai asks.

"Get your heads on straight. Rialynne is off limits." Xander growls.

"I don't take orders from you, Xander. If I want her, I am damn well going to have her." Jett snarls before walking away.

"I should go after Rialynne." Kai says before walking away.

"What's wrong with you?" I ask Xander. He sighs before rubbing his hand on the back of his neck.

"We can't fuck this up. She is a distraction we do not need. I cannot fail him." I was not sure if he meant King Roderick or his father.

"I hear you, but you need to understand. We are all kings and I respect you but stop trying to take charge of us. We have worked as one unit since the beginning. Jett will never agree to not go after something he wants. I know my cousin."

"Fine, but don't say I didn't warn all of you. If the king finds out, we will all be dead." Xander walks away from me to go mingle with nobles. Looking around, I see Jett sulking in the shadows with a drink in his hand, while I try to figure out what the hell all this means. Four souls calling on the same one has never been heard of. If her soul has called to one of ours, then that would leave a mark on the three she didn't choose.

Fated mates is something that is usually common within species, not interracial. Humans and Blood Elfs do not mate. It is permitted for them to marry, if the marriage is blessed by a king. The only relationship that has worked out like that is my aunt and Jett's Uncle.

In all technicality, we share no blood. We are only cousins, but I grew up around him. Both of us being rogues is one of the other qualities we have in common. Our mission and secret alliance with King Roderick strengthened our bond and formed one with Xander and Kai. All our parents were killed at the same time. Except for Xander's father.

He is the last of our parents' generation still alive. I can see the stress and guilt that Xander carries with him daily. The duties of being a king takes time away from family. The illness his father is fighting is one that is incurable and painful. I feel for my friend. I know what it means to grieve the loss of a parent.

The door opening has me snapping out of my stupor just as her scent catches in my breath.

Rialynne Faith is my soul mate, and no one will keep me from fighting for her.

Chapter Four

KAI

I race outside, searching for my fiancée. Only to find her looking out at the night sky, over a railing. I try not to let my gaze wander down to her curves, but I cannot help it.

When I caught her scent, it was as if a part of my soul recognized her. I do not know how, being that I am a human, but I will not be able to let her go. Not completely. A part of me needs to know if she felt the same but since she had a negative reaction to me, I suspect she does not.

I watch her for a few moments, trying to figure out what she might be thinking. When her initial reaction was to question the fact that I am a human and a rogue, I admit it hurt. I can understand her disgust against my Order, seeing as it was a rogue that killed her mother and attacked her.

She doesn't seem to have been affected at all physically by that day as far as I can tell from looking at her. From our dance, I got a close look at her beautiful face and saw no scars, only the painful emotion deep within her bright green irises.

When her body molded to mine as I guided us across the dance floor, I knew I wouldn't be able to let her go.

The perfect curve of her body, the way we danced in-sync with one another, spoke volumes about our compatibility. If only she would be able to see past my Order. Would her father bless a real marriage between us? I would like to think my devotion and loyalty over the years has earned me the right to ask for his daughter's hand.

That is if she even wants to marry you.

Clearing my throat, I allow myself a moment to breathe before speaking her name.

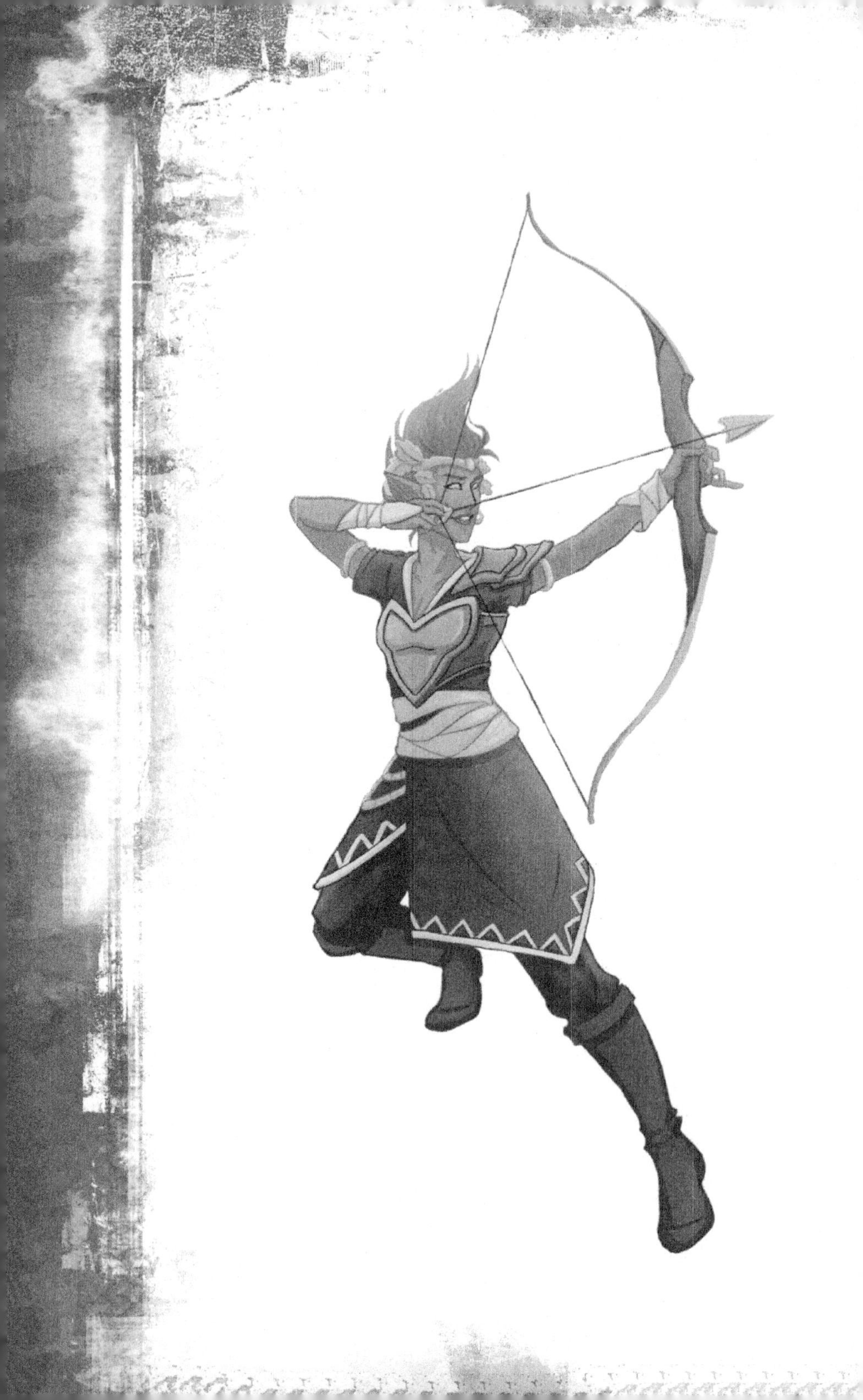

Chapter Five

RIALYNNE

A deep voice laced with concern hits me the same time the scent of seafoam washes over me. He followed me.

"I want to be alone." I say without turning to speak to him.

"It isn't safe for you to be out here unchaperoned." The anxiety turns to anger at the comment. Turning, I get caught in Kai's gaze for a moment but snap out of it.

"Why? Because I am a woman? You think I cannot protect myself?" I ask him. Clenching my fists and trying to keep my power from seeping out of my skin.

Your power is tied to your emotions, little red. You mustn' allow them to show, or your life will be in more danger than it already is. Master Runk's wise words echo in my ears and my heart clenches with his memory.

"Yes," he states, as he clasps his hands behind his back. He steps towards me. I stand my ground and at the last moment he steps to my side. Looking over the arched gazebo at the vast nursery of flowers and plants. "And no." His last word surprises me.

"What does that mean?" I ask, turning to stand next to him, putting a good double-arm length of space between us.

"It means that a beautiful woman like yourself, with the status of a royal, is not safe from an attack." I do not look at him, but I see the logic in his words. "But I would be foolish to believe that you are untrained in self-defense. Especially being the ward of our great king."

King Sarrs is not the one who took it upon himself to train me in the art, nor did he ever condone it.

I raise my head to the sky, closing my eyes, a small breeze raising goosebumps along my exposed skin. Usually, I would just use my fire to keep me warm, but I cannot with Kai standing near me. He would see and that would be something I cannot explain. Nor do I want to.

"Are you cold?" he asks, and I realize he moved closer. Not close enough to touch me, but when I open my eyes, I get caught in his gaze. The deepest shade of blue I have ever seen. Reminding me of the depths of the midnight sky. If I am not careful, I may get lost and never find my way back again.

"Excuse me," a male's voice breaks our moment and we both turn to see a king's guard standing just outside the arched opening. Dressed in the finest crimson armor from helm to boot. The crest of Klestria emblazoned upon his chest plate. "I was instructed to guard the queen."

"Do you think her fiancé is incapable of this task?" I hear Kai ask, and I turn away to hide my blush. "Or do you think the queen cannot defend herself?"

He asks the same question I asked him, and it baffles me. When I catch his eye, he gives me a smirk that reveals a dimple on his right cheek and then winks at me.

"No. Sire, but it isn't safe for Queen Rialynne to be out here alone." The guard responds.

"Does it look like she is alone?"

"No, sire." He responds. If I do not step in, Kai might have this guard pissing in his pants.

"Thank you, you may post right outside the gardens. If I need you, I will simply scream in fright." I tell the guard and he hesitates briefly before bowing and moving to his post.

"Wow." Kai states with a whistle.

"What?"

"I wish I had power like that." His statement confuses me.

"You are a King of Zavinia. You have power." I remind him, not believing that he thinks I somehow have more.

"Apparently not as much as you." He states with a shrug of his shoulders before walking back to the railing overlooking the garden.

"I do not have power here." I whisper before moving to stand next to him. Leaving just more than a foot of space between us.

"I highly doubt that my queen." There he goes again with those two words. A shiver runs along my spine again this time not because of the cool breeze, but instead because of the reality of those words. I am to be his queen.

When I do not respond, he moves closer. Still giving me space, but not as much as I would like. I sidestep and move further away from him. Kai smirks at me but does not move again. Silently respecting my decision. After a few minutes of listening to the nature of the night, I sigh.

"I guess we should head back before they send out more guards." I state and then turn to walk. Kai grips my elbow, stopping me, the contact of his fingers, makes my skin heat.

"Rialynne," I look at him, then down to where he is holding my arm, then back to his face. I watch as his eyes go from mine to my lips then back up. "I'm sorry."

"For what?" I ask him barely above a whisper. He drops his hand and I instantly miss his warmth.

"I know this is not what you want." He answers.

"What makes you say that?" I need to know if he can read my emotions, because I cannot read him.

"The part where you ran away the second you got a chance." A flash of pain crosses his eyes but quickly fades.

"We should head back." *This is not an appropriate time for this conversation.*

I state before turning and beginning to walk, grateful he did not stop me this time. I hear his footsteps following me, and I nod to the guard as I pass him, stopping just outside the entrance to the ballroom that connects to the garden.

"Shall we?" He says, reaching out for me to take his arm. I do, and heat prickles along my skin again where we are connected. We push through the doors and are instantly greeted with chatter, music, and dancing.

As we make our way to the front, we stop every so often to accept congratulations from various patrons.

"Congratulations, Your Majesties." Says a burly male human with a gut made of alcohol, covered in the emerald fabrics of Magianinasphere.

"Thank you, Lord Tumbers." Kai states with a pearly white smile painted on his face. I wonder if his cheeks are as sore as mine from all the fake smiles we are obligated to make while conversing with the Lords and Ladies of Zavinia.

"You must visit us in Hitachi. I will provide you with the best timber and produce in all Zavinia. Surely your kitchens will be grateful for the fresh vegetables and fruits." Lord Tumbers states through missing teeth. It takes me by surprise, but I notice a scar coming across his cheek, showing the result of some sort of fight.

Lords are not usually as unfit as this one. They are trained from the moment they can walk to wield weapons and take care of their bodies. Males fight our wars, although the only enemy we have these days are assassins and rebels. All fighting in the name of the king and queen of old. A time when Zavinia was one continent instead of five.

Master Runk and the ladies of the Cathedral went on and on about the time of old kings and queens. When females were highly regarded and permitted to fight instead of staying behind with the wounded. But everything changed when the king went insane and started murdering civilians.

King Sarrs started a rebellion to save us. The old king was the strongest elemental with the ability to wield all four elements. He was known as the last Elite Elemental. It was on his last breath that he cursed our world and divided the five territories. I do not know when the transition of female warriors to female housewives occurred.

"We will have to check our schedule and see if our tour will go through the village." Kai answers, his voice snapping me out of my daze. "It is time we move forward. It is customary for us to speak with the other kings."

"Of course." Lord Tumbers bows, and we follow suit before making our way towards the front.

"Are you okay?" Kai whispers.

"Yes." I answer with a smile.

He stops suddenly, leaning forward and whispering in my ear.

"One of these days, you will learn to trust me." More heat rushing against my skin at the closeness of his body. He retracts before I can say or do anything, we move forward.

The scent of fire and ash surround me as we step up to greet the King of the north. King Enzo Covaxs, fire elemental human rogue. "Congratulations." He states with a sneer.

"Thank you." Kai states. I watch their intense stare-off. Enzo's gaze shifts to me, my breath catches when his eyes, like warm chocolate, catch me. A new sensation hits me as the hairs on the back of my neck raise.

Danger.

A smirk forms at the left corner of his mouth at the noticeable reaction my body gives off.

"Queen Rialynne Faith, what a pleasure to meet you. At last." He reaches out to take my hand and I watch as he raises it to his lips and brushes the softest kiss upon my knuckles. The amber color of his eyes flash over red for the briefest of moments. A kiss of fire rushes over me as he releases me.

"The honor is all mine, King Enzo Covaxs." *What is wrong with me? All I have been doing is getting speechless and heated around these males. Master Runk taught me better than this. Get your shit together.* I smirk at him back, sending a wave of water magic under my skin to cool it from his touch. It goes unnoticed, which is a relief. I catch Kai giving me a raised brow as we move to the next king.

The scent of pine and earth wash over me as we step in front of King Xander Zain.

The earth elemental mage of the Magianinasphere. A blood elf, one that I thought would take me as his bride instead of a human. His dark skin is flawless and is complimented with the green color of his knee length tunic. A staff is positioned in his left hand. Typical for a mage, they always carry their staff.

"My Queen," Xander bows slightly, his words catching me off-guard.

"My King," I say and bow back. Kai's grip on my arm tightens and I look at him.

He is angry.

For what I am not sure.

"You are an incredibly lucky man, Kai. To be engaged to the most beautiful woman in all of Zavinia." Xander's words bring a blush into my cheeks and my core clenches with the flattery.

"Thank you for your unnecessary compliment, King Xander. I am sure there are just as, if not more beautiful women in this realm. In fact, I know of many." I dare a glance at Kai, who seems to be on the verge of breaking his composure. I notice his jaw is clenched. He is not just angry, he is pissed.

"Your humility is humbling, my Queen." I notice Kai's jaw clenches even tighter, he must be mad at Xander, but why? He is simply being nice. "I would like to welcome you and King Kai to my palace in Magianinasphere if you ever get a chance. You know the timber in our land is the best, something I don't think comes easy to the swamps of the Oceaniansphere."

Ouch.

"I'm sure the Oceaniansphere is more than capable of providing the necessary resources needed for our people." Kai speaks and there is ice in his tone. Xander's dark eyes do not leave mine when he responds.

"If you ever find yourself needing anything or if you feel the Oceaniansphere is not meeting your every need, my doors are always open." Xander states and then winks at me. Goddess be damned.

"Xander, I don't think you should be trying to take Kai's fiancée before they have had a chance to get acquainted." Another deep voice, with a slight southern territory accent catches my ears. The scent of air and snow washed over me. I turn and my breath catches at the sight of the most stunning blood elf male I have ever laid eyes on.

Hair the color of raven feathers and eyes the shade of sapphires, King Jett Covaxs takes the same hand his cousin kissed and brushes his soft lips over the spot.

"You must forgive Xander for his brashness, it's very unbecoming." Jett states and I notice my hand is still in his.

"Right, of course." I say taking my hand back. This is all too much for me. The testosterone surrounding me is beginning to suffocate me and I feel as though I may pass out.

"Are you okay, my queen?" A deep voice states and I am not sure who said it this time.

Kai maybe?

"She looks pale." Xander maybe?

"Shit, catch her." Strong arms wrap around me as my vision fades and darkness consumes me.

"Run a little red, run fast, fly high, and never look back." Master Runk says, as he draws his sword from his waist.

"Not without you." I say in a panic.

"Remember your training." I nod and feel my power surge as I conjure my bow and arrows. Aiming, I focus on my first mark. Dark shadows cloud them from my vision but as I call upon my inner power, I see through it.

"You will not escape this time."

My arrow sails straight at its target, hitting it directly in the arm. It turns and growls. It is the most terrifying sound I have ever heard.

"Run, little red." Master Rank's voice booms, but I am frozen in place. My power failed me at the memory of the last time I heard that noise. The last time I heard my mother's soft voice and felt my father's warm touch. My vision fades and in an instant, I am crouched behind the throne where my father usually sat.

"You don't need to do this." My father's pleading voice comes from in front of me. "She is just a child."

"No, she isn't, and you know it," a masked voice booms.

"You cannot have her." My Mother's voice hits my ears and suddenly everything that was scaring me vanishes. "You will have to kill us first."

"No." I hear myself say as I come out from the throne. I cannot see the masked male. Screams and magic erupt all around us as my head hits metal and everything suddenly goes silent.

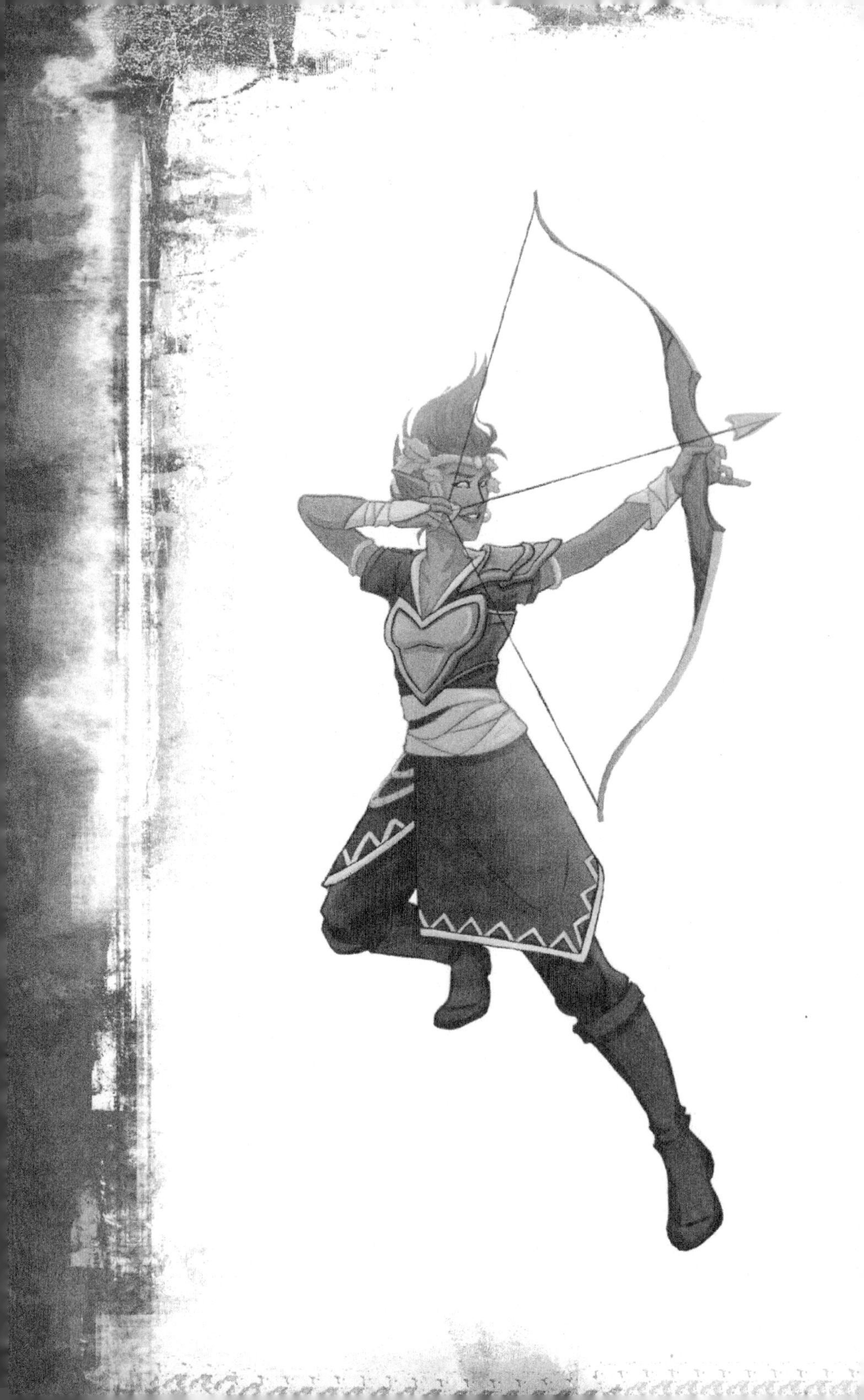

Chapter Six

RIALYNNE

"She is waking up, give her some space." Lady Willow states and when my eyes open, I see the ceiling of my room, back at the Cathedral. I sit up and my head pounds. "Easy, my child."

"What happened?" I look down and notice I am still in my ball gown.

"You fainted." Kai's voice comes from the darkest corner of my room.

Embarrassment floods me and I bring my knees to my chest.

"Oh, sorry." I state and take a chalice of water from Lady Willow. Kai moves forward and comes to my bedside. Lady Willow looks between the two of us as she rises to her feet and excusing herself from the room.

"Are you okay?" he asks with concern covering his entire face.

"Yes, not sure why I fainted." I answer truthfully.

"When was the last time you drank?" His question surprises me and

I try to think about it. Usually, I do not need to drink, except when I use my powers, much like all blood elfs.

"I don't remember, but I don't need to. I don't have power." I am trying to keep up the lie I have told since I was a child. No one must know I have magic. Father used to say that more than once a day as I was growing up.

"You are still a blood elf, which means you still need it sometimes." He was right about that. The very nature of our being is that we need to feed our bloodlust every month to suppress the monster that lies beneath us. Part of the rogue rebellion is full of those elfs driven by bloodlust. There are also unfortunate souls who die because their body is completely drained of blood.

Only humans though, never elfs. It is forbidden to drink from one another, just as it is to drink directly from the vein of a human.

"I am fine, I had some a few weeks ago during my monthly bleed." I instantly cover my mouth at the very intimate detail I just revealed to him, and he chuckles.

"Do not be embarrassed. I am to be your husband and a female's monthly bleed is natural. It means you could bear children if you chose to." He smiles and I cannot help but smile back. "Are you sure you are, okay? I can give you..."

"Give me, what?" I ask as my heart rate increases and he moves closer.

"A taste." He whispers as his eyes move to my lips again, telling me that he wants to kiss me.

"It's forbidden." I tell him, but he inches closer.

"Not when you are my wife." He reaches up to cup my cheek, but I flinch. "I will not hurt you."

"You cannot. We are not wed yet." I remind him. He moves closer, his fingertips brushing against my arm causing me to gasp.

A knock sounds and he breaks his contact. I get to my feet the same as him and we walk to the door in silence. On the other side, I see three familiar faces.

"We came to check on the queen." Xander states and something stirs inside me. Worry? Fear? Curiosity? Desire? I look at Kai with confusion and he looks like he is ready to fight the three kings for their intrusion.

"I am fine-" but before I could finish, all three pushed inside and I found myself standing in my room alone with four kings.

What the fuck is going on?

"She said she is fine." Kai states stepping between me and the rest.

"Why don't you let her speak for herself?" Enzo states stepping up to face Kai.

"Are you all serious right now?" I ask, but Kai and Enzo do not stop staring at one another. I notice both have magic at their fingertips. Fire and water. Opposite of each other.

"We are just concerned for you, my queen." Xander states taking a step towards me and that breaks Kai's eye contact as he moves up to Xander.

"Stop calling her that." He growls, sounding very animalistic. I feel myself moving backwards until my bed is separating me and the four males.

"Why? Are you afraid she will come to me instead of you?" Xander teases, and I do not understand what the big deal is.

"She is my fiancé, which means I am the only one who gets to call her that." Kai growls, and I feel myself getting angry at the immaturity of these males. It does not make a lick of sense to me what any of them call me. I am a queen, so what does it matter?

"And that means you are the only one who gets to claim her as his queen?" Jett speaks this time. Three against one and I am starting to get worried that something bad might happen if I do not stop them.

"Why don't we ask her what she wants to be called?" Enzo asks and all four pairs of eyes land on me. Suddenly, I feel exceedingly small, and my power pushes at the edge of my skin. I close my eyes and breathe.

1.. 2.. 3.. 4.. 5.. 6.. 7. 8.. 9.. 10.

QUEEN OF KINGS

"I would like you all to leave." I state without looking at any of them.

"Not until you tell us what we are permitted to call you." Enzo states and then I snap my eyes to all of them. I will not allow these males to try and intimidate or control me.

"I said get the fuck out of my room. Now." I growl and clench my fists, controlling my power before it spills out of me. All four of them seem momentarily speechless. "Five...four...three..."

"As you command, my queen." Xander bows with a wink and leaves first. Kai is the last to leave, giving me a look of concern. When my door shuts, I release my power, using it to lock my door and add a barrier. My head pounds and I know I need to feed. Straining and exhausting my efforts to keep my power on lock is draining me.

Walking over to my dresser, I pull open the bottom drawer and withdraw a crystal vase filled with the crimson liquid. My mouth waters at the sight of it and I take a sip, letting the copper tang flow down my throat and refuel me. Capping it, I place it back in my drawer and close it.

I move to my bathroom and rinse the last of the blood from my mouth. "That was a close one Ria, we need to be more careful." I sigh. My skin tingles with the memory of each of their touches. The soft and tender brush of Kai, the fire of Enzo, the rush teasing nature of Xander, and the coolness of Jett. Four males and all four of them make my core clench with a need I have never felt before.

Running the icy water, I splash my face, completely disregarding my make-up as the black charcoal runs from my eyes. I clutch the necklace and then bring it to my lips. The diamond was a gift from Master Runk when I was sixteen.

"I fainted today. I almost let my power go. Forgive me, Master. I will do better." I like talking to my necklace. It feels as though I can be closer to him. A knock sounds. Before I move, I use my air magic to dry my face and fix my cosmetics quickly. When I see who it is, I roll my eyes.

"Didn't you get the hint?" I stop speaking when Kai's finger moves to my lips. I begin to get angry, but he gives me a look that says he is serious. I nod and he gestures for me to follow him.

We move down the corridor, towards the ball room and I wonder if he is just trying to get me to come back to the ball but then I hear it. The same noise that has haunted me since the night I lost my parents. The horrid screeching. The growl. The scent of blood and death. Kai pushes me against the wall.

Pressing his body to mine, sending all kinds of sensations exploding across my skin. *'Stay silent and keep moving.'* He mouths to me. I nod. His hands are on my hips, and I get lost in the moment as my eyes move to his lips. I look back at him and he gives me a knowing smirk.

"Am I interrupting something?" Jett's voice comes from beside us. His sword and a spot on his cheek is covered in black blood. Kai steps back from me and I tuck a strand of hair behind my ear.

"I was just telling my queen to stay silent and keep moving." Kai growls putting an emphasis on the words, my queen. Ignoring him, I walk up to Jett and tear a part of my sash to clean his cheek. He flinches at the small gesture and our eyes lock momentarily. The scent of him washes over me. I am entrapped in his gaze. His eyes are so mesmerizing that I feel like I could stare into them all day.

"Thank you," he says just above a whisper.

"Can't have you walking around with blood on your face. It isn't very kingly." I state and then step back.

"We need to get her to safety." Kai growls, taking my elbow and pulling me to him. "Do you know a way out of here that isn't through the ball room?"

"Yes, we can go through the servants' quarters."

"Lead the way," he tells me. At first, I am nervous, but the distant noise of screams and fighting urges me forward.

"What about the people? We should be fighting with them." I tell them.

"You are a queen, Rialynne, not a warrior." Kai states.

"You know nothing about me." I growl and shove past him. I do not stop as I pick up speed and run towards the ball room. I will not cower in the face of danger. When I burst through the doors, I see blood and death all around me. Black figures fighting against the people of Zavinia. Without thought, I conjure my quiver of arrows and bow.

Knocking them one at a time, I take down as many as I can before I am knocked to my feet by a powerful gust of wind.

"Where have you been hiding?" A muffled voice of one of the rebels' barks as he approaches me. His brown eyes are glaring at me with hate. I cannot see the rest of his face underneath the cloth, but I get to my feet and square up with him as he steps in front of me with his double blades. "That is cute, a female trying to fight. Do not hurt yourself, love. Just get on your knees where you belong."

In a split second, I knock an arrow and aim for the spot between his eyes. He starts laughing maniacally and I let my arrow fly. He catches it right as it pierces his skin, a trickle of blood coming down the center. He growls and charges, punching me in the ribs. I double-over as I feel them crack and my vision starts to falter.

Thick fingers wrap around my throat and begin to squeeze as I scratch and stare at his arm. "You bitch! You almost killed me."

"That's the point." I growl as he squeezes harder. When I feel my body weakening from the lack of oxygen, he smiles. Suddenly, a crunching sound rings in my ears as blood spatters on my face and the rebel's head rolls from his shoulders. I am dropped to the floor, coughing, and gasping for air.

"Breathe, Red, breathe." Jett is standing there, helping me to my feet. "We need to leave."

"I can't abandon my people." I croak.

His blue eyes are full of understanding.

"And I can't let you die." He nods before forcing me to my feet. "Xander, get us out of here." I look at the mage king with pleading eyes, but he shakes his head before summoning a portal. A swirling vortex of blue sucks me in and I feel myself free falling.

When I land on the other side, the contents of my stomach come out and coat the snow-covered ground. A hand is on my back rubbing it, while another pulls my hair back to ensure I do not get vomit in it.

"First time?" Xander asks, as I get to my feet, wiping my mouth. Kai was holding my hair, while Jett rubbed my back. I look around, suddenly searching for my fire king. *No, not my fire king.*

"Water?" Enzo's voice comes from behind me, and I smell his scent. I turn around and grip the waterskin, gulping it down before rinsing my mouth out. I look around and notice we are in the middle of a forest of snow-covered evergreens, which means we are in either Jett or Enzo's territory. Not sure which one since both climates are the same.

"Why the fuck did you bring me here?" I growl at Xander, who seems taken aback at my brash words.

"I just saved us." He snaps, stepping up to me. I had to look up at him, but I do not care.

"You should be more grateful, Ria."

"Don't call me that."

"Or what? Ria," He teases, and I bring my fists up and connect directly with his jaw. His eyes flash green as he looks back at me before spitting his blood to the ground.

"Feisty. I like it. But I shouldn't be surprised by a queen with power such as you."

Shit.

"Did you think we wouldn't notice you conjuring arrows out of mid-air?" Enzo asks from next to me.

"What was that Rialynne? We were told you had no powers." Kai asks. I look around at all four of them, my breathing becoming harder, and I feel a panic attack is coming. It has not happened in a while, but I cannot breathe.

They are around me, closing in.

My power.

They know, and now they will kill me for it.

"Step back," Kai warns, but it's too late. My powers engulf my body, green flames dancing around me as I try to reign in my control. I see nothing. I feel nothing. I cannot breathe, my chest is caving in on itself.

"Look at me." I lock onto two blue eyes, and I feel the cool rush of air kissing my skin. "Breathe with me, Red." Jett is cupping my face and willing me to breathe. "In and out." I feel the tears running down my cheeks, but it does not sting like I expected it too. My body begins to fatigue, and I feel myself falling but a strong-arm wraps around my waist, scooping me up to cradle me. I bury my face into his chest, breathing in the cool frosted scent of Jett.

"It was a panic attack." Jett says and I close my eyes. "She is fine, but we cannot crowd her. Build a shelter, I got her."

I peek out and notice no protest and the others begin to build a place for the evening. "You okay, Red?"

I look up at him and my fingers itch to run them through his beard. I stop myself, thinking it would be too intimate.

"Yeah." I answer and he lowers me to my feet. I let go of him and then step back. "I'm sorry."

"Don't." he waves me off. "You have nothing to apologize for. We should have never crowded you like that."

"I need to walk." I tell him and he nods.

"Alone."

"I can't do that," he rubs the back of his neck. "But I will allow you a head start."

"Thank you." I begin walking towards the direction of the moon. The snow crunches under my boots and I try to recall everything that has been going on. The engagement. The fainting. The four kings. The attack. My power.

"Forgive me, Master. I failed." I fall to my knees, hugging myself as I begin to cry. I cup my face in my hands before screaming into the sky. Letting all my anger and regret burst out of me. A tremor of green blasts across the land making the trees bend.

"Red?" I turn and see Jett with his hand on the hilt of his sword with an air shield around him. Getting to my feet, I instantly conjure my bow and arrows and aim it at him. He puts his hands up in a movement of surrender. "I'm not going to hurt you."

"How do I know?" I ask not wanting to believe him.

"Don't you think that if I wanted to kill you, you would already be dead?" He is right, but I just can't let myself trust them. Not after what they saw me do. Why can't I control my powers around them?

"You saw me. You know." I state and then the other three show up. All lined up with their hands raised and concerned washes over their features. I pull three more arrows, four all together knocked and ready to go if necessary.

"If you think I cannot hit you all at once, you will be mistaken."

"Ria, we aren't going to hurt you. Please just talk to us." Xander states.

"Listen to us, Rialynne. We just saved you." Kai states.

"We swear on Ares, we will not harm you." Enzo pleads, but I cannot seem to drop my arms.

"I cannot trust you. I don't know any of you and none of you know me." I growl.

"Then get to know us." Jett reasons. "We will make an oath to the goddess. If we break it, we die." The others do not even flinch, and my gut tells me to trust him, but my brain says otherwise. And then my traitorous heart tells me something else. Something that I will not allow itself to voice.

"Vow you will never lie to me or betray me." I seem to command without stuttering. They all bring their right fists over their hearts and vow it. I lower my arms, returning my arrows, but keeping my bow at the ready.

"Will you come back to camp, Ria?" Xander asks and I do not know if I like him using that nickname. I nod, and then follow them. Once we step foot into the camp, I notice a large fire is at the center and five tents made of ice are built. Thank the goddess I got my own.

We all take seats along logs around the fire. Jett and Kai on either side of me, while Xander and Enzo sit across the fire. "Why didn't you just let me die?"

"This doesn't make sense-because we aren't as heartless as the rumors portray us." Kai states.

"But what I am is against the laws." I mutter.

"True but they are against King Sarrs laws not ours." Kai states and I look between all four of them and a revelation comes to mind.

"Wait a minute. Are all four of you allies?" I ask in disbelief.

"We all have an understanding." Xander states.

"Why? I mean, it does not make sense to me. Wouldn't three of you be less powerful than the one that is married to me? I figured that would tear our world further apart."

"It would." Kai states but not smugly.

"You aren't married." Enzo growls. "We are all of equal power."

"Yet." Kai states. I get to my feet.

"You seriously think it is still appropriate for us to get married?" I ask him.

"Yes, you are my queen. Why shouldn't I want to marry you?" He states as he gets to his feet. Then out of the corner of my eye, I see the other three.

"Because" I stammer, not sure how to argue it.

"I think we should allow Rialynne to decide who her king gets to be." Enzo states and Kai growls.

"No, she is mine." Kai states.

"I don't belong to anyone." I tell him. "I will not choose." I storm past Kai, jamming my shoulder into his and straight into my tent. Using my earth magic to slam the door shut. I worry for a moment about using it out in the public eye, but then decide to forget it because they have already seen me conjure. I hear distant curses and then someone agrees on a watch rotation. I settle into the makeshift bed, using my fire magic to keep me warm.

    They only know I have powers; they do not know I am an Elite. They do not know I am a Druid. I fear that if they do, they will kill me.

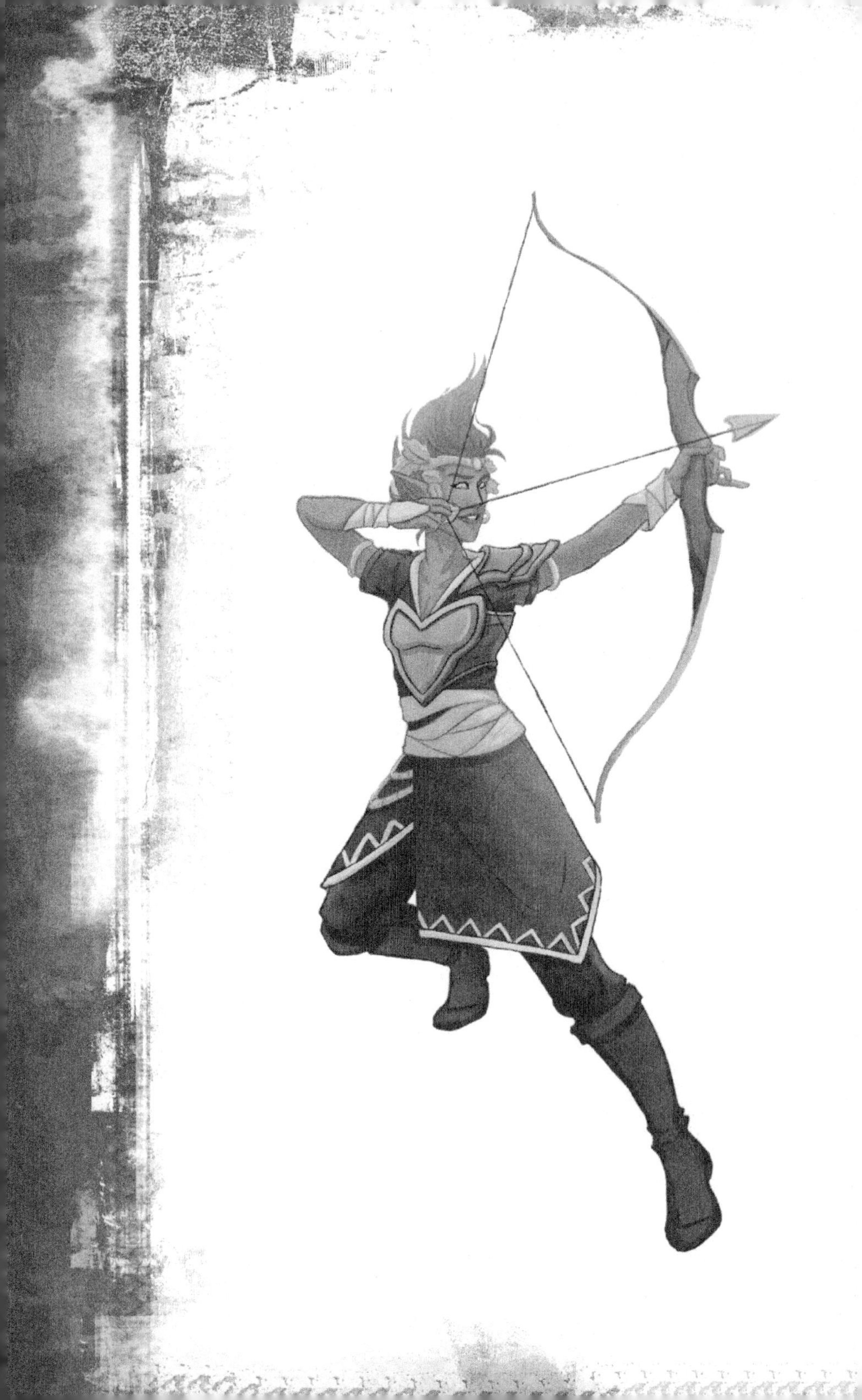

Chapter Seven

RIALYNNE

Morning dawned and brought with it a blizzard with relentless gale winds and hail. In the middle of the night, we morphed one giant shelter for all five of us to share to prepare for the oncoming storm. I have my own room, along with the others. With mine and Xander's combined earth magic, we morphed a two-level shelter of ice.

The top level meant for our rooms, the bottom housed a living room and makeshift bathroom. Enzo used his fire magic to heat some snow for bathing.

While I soak in the steamy water, I use my own fire magic to keep it warm while using my earth and water magic to keep the bathroom intact.

Using my magic freely feels so right but it is also terrifyingly addicting. The sensation of getting caught adds to the heat of my body. I must keep my emotions in check if I am going to survive this.

I clutch the diamond necklace and kiss it once more before getting out of the bath. I use my air magic to dry myself off and then fire warm my skin. Enzo managed to bring clothing with us when we escaped, saying he is always prepared for any situation that arises. Undergarments, however, are something which he did not think of. Undoing my white sash, I wrap it around my breasts to add some type of support before pulling on a crimson tunic.

Next, I try to think of what I can use for underwear, before deciding that I can just go without seeing as I have leggings. I pull on the clean ivory pair and then pull up a crimson skirt. All made of wool and compliment my dark complexion. There is no mirror, I cannot really check to make sure I am good to go, before I exit the bathroom.

All eyes land on me and any noise becomes suddenly quiet. My cheeks heat from embarrassment and I make my way to the stairs made of ice before heading up my room and shutting the door. Goddesses help me.

I put my dirty clothes into a pile at the edge of the makeshift bed before sitting on it and placing my face in my palms. "What the fuck am I doing here? With four fucking kings that all look ready to pounce with all their alpha-hole energy."

"Red," Jett's voice catches my ears on the outside of the door. I look up and move to it.

"I brought some breakfast if you are hungry."

I sigh, my stomach grumbling at the mention of food and then open the door. His airy scent washes over me as he smiles at me, revealing his sharpened canines. My own tingle with the sensation of another blood elf so close. I need to drink. I used more magic than I am used to.

"Thank you," I say, opening the door just enough to take a bowl of fruit from him. He stands there and stares at me again. Something I seem to be doing with him. Getting lost in each other's eyes. "Do you want to come in?"

Why would I ask him that? Please say no. Please say no.

"Sure, if you don't mind?" He smiles and I open the door further for him. The door closes behind him and I take a deep breath before placing the bowl on top of the table that is across from my bed. I pull out a chair, take a seat, then pop a strawberry in my mouth. It's so sweet and I cover my mouth to hide the juice I am sure is dripping from my jaw.

"Here, allow me." When I expect him to hand me a cloth, I am stunned when the pad of his tongue licks the juices from my chin. "Delicious."

"You could've given me a napkin." I told him.

"True, but where is the fun in that?" he winks sitting across from me. Not sure how to respond to that, I took a blueberry and ate it. "How are you?"

"Are you asking if I am going to have another panic attack? Because the answer is no." I see some tension relief from his shoulders. When my head begins to pound, I place my palm on it.

"You okay, Red?" Jett asks.

"Just a headache, I will be fine." I told him.

"You need to feed." I do not respond because I highly doubt, they have blood out here that is not from the vein.

"No, I had some last night before the attack." I tell him but he moves to me before biting into his wrists.

"You need fresh blood." I shake my head.

"It's dangerous and forbidden." I have grown up hearing about the stories of those who drink from another. They become addicted, driven by bloodlust. It's too intimate.

"Just as forbidden as a female elemental?" he asks, and the scent of his blood makes my mouth water. "Drink. If not from me, then one of them."

I continue to shake my head and backup until I am pressed against the wall. "I can't."

He growls before pressing his hand over his wrists and healing it. He moves forward, placing a hand either side of my head, "One of these days you will drink from me. When you allow yourself to let go, you will be rewarded with pleasure and power you don't yet know is possible."

"Is everything okay?" Kai's voice comes in a growl and Jett steps back.

"Yes, just making sure Red ate her breakfast." He walks away and I feel myself missing his warmth.

"You okay, Ria?" Kai asks me and I look at him. Concern coating his features and then I walk to him. I do not know why but I feel safe with him. I cup his face, running my fingers through his beard, allowing myself to feel the silk and coarse mixture of it. "Ria,"

"I'm fine." I step back. "Sorry." I turn and bolt out of my room, down the steps and out the front door straight into the blizzard. I form an air shield around me as I begin to run. I do not stop until I come across a frozen lake. Looking up at the sky, unable to see through the downpour of snow and hail.

"What is wrong with me?!" I scream. Knowing there is no one that will hear me. I close my eyes and clutch my necklace wishing I could talk to Master Runk again.

"Look at me." Warm hands cup my face and I see but cannot believe my old Master standing in front of me.

"Master?" I ask.

"It's me, little red. Have you forgotten everything I taught you?" he asks.

"No, but I failed to keep my power under control. The four kings, they know. But they have not killed me yet. They seem to be enamored but that isn't possible." He chuckles and my heart squeezes at the familiar sound.

"You have forgotten one of my most important lessons, child." I look at him confused. "Do you remember the story I told you about the fae goddess?" I nod.

"It was some fairytale about fated mates."

"It wasn't just a fairytale. It is real. They are exceedingly rare and far in between but once you have found your fated mate, there is an unbreakable bond formed. An attraction and an overwhelming need to protect them."

"I don't have that. Not with any of them. I am just a power piece to them." I told him.

"No, Rialynne you are not." My vision fades and I hear his words and cannot believe them. In the spot where he was standing, a figure comes into view. That morphs into four different forms. The kings. *My* kings.

"Red," I hear Jett yelling.

"Rialynne," Enzo yells. And my heart pounds. They came to find me. They barely know me and are risking themselves to come find me. Getting to my feet, I look around for a place to hide because I cannot go back to them. They will not be safe around me. Turning on my heel, I run.

I hear the pounding of footsteps behind me as my air shield protects me. My magic is quickly fading, and fatigue is starting to settle. I am not used to using my magic like this.

"Red, stop." Jett yells from somewhere behind me. I continue to run until I am sliding across the frozen lake and then stop in the middle.

Shit.

The cracking sound begins all around me, I use my water and earth magic to try and keep it solid under me, but I am too late. A thousand knives pierce my skin as I am swallowed by the rush of the current. My throat and lungs are on fire as I try to calm myself, but nothing is working.

I am tapped out on magic and my vision fades. My last thought is, *I am going to die-*

"Wake up, Red." Air pushes into my lungs as water is pulled out. Coughing, I gasp for air, but it is not as difficult as it should be. I open my eyes to see the familiar faces of Kai and Jett. One of black hair and pointed ears and the other of dirty blonde hair and rounded ears.

"Kai, Jett." My voice croaks.

"We're here, Red. Just breathe in and out. Enzo, she needs warmth." Heat melts the ice from my bones, and I look down to see the fire rogue touching my ankle.

"What the fuck were you thinking?" Xander growls. "You could've died."

"Chill out, man." Kai scolds him. I look around and notice a large air shield is around us and we are on a bank of snow next to the frozen lake.

"You should've let me." I tell them and all four kings freeze in place. "Then I would no longer be a threat to you or our realm."

"Is that what you think you are?" Kai asks, his voice laced with pain.

"I know you are all thinking about it. A female with the power of the elements. Not just that, the ability to conjure my own arrows." Then I just realized I said elements and not element.

"You are an Elite." Jett states more than asks and I nod thinking fuck it. If I am going to die, at least someone should know.

"What is your Order?" Kai asks. "Are you a mage, hunter, warrior, or rogue?" I know why he is asking because rogues are usually loyal to other rogues, but I am none of those.

"None of the above." I tell him and then scan their faces.

"Not possible." Xander growls. "You can conjure weapons out of thin air. You must be a mage. The only other order that can do that doesn't exist anymore."

"What order is that?" Enzo asks. I know I might regret this but, might as well come clean about this. If Master Runk is correct, and one of these men is my mate, then they should know the truth.

"Druids." I answer him and they all look back at me. "I am a druid. The last of my kind. Just like my parents."

"How the hell did you get away with that?" Xander asks. "There is a test done."

The test that the earth mage is referring to is the one that is conducted during your infant stage. Monks come forth to every newborn and test them with each element and order. By placing the symbols of all four in front of you. Each symbol has a relic of old that is blessed by Ares herself. If your power calls onto one of the elements, then that is your Elemental. The same goes with Orders.

"I don't know, I just know that I am." I tell him, sitting up. Kai looks at me and then speaks.

"We should continue this discussion back at camp. We will all need to replenish our magic soon." We all agree and head back.

The walk back was silent, and I soon realized I did not make it that far from our camp. Once inside, Enzo warms the area quickly as we take a seat on the couch. Kai and Jett sit on either side of me, seeming to not want me out of their sight, in case I run off again.

"Tell us everything." Kai states.

"Master Runk taught me from the moment my parents died that I came from a generation of Druid Elites. I have the power to wield all four elements and conjure anything I desire without reciting spells or incantations like the mages, but also, I can shapeshift into any creature I can imagine." I look around to see if anyone will interrupt but none do.

"When my parents were assassinated, Master Runk made a point to train me. I learned how to wield my powers as well as self-defense. But I also had to hide it all because if King Sarrs found out, I would be executed."

"Not going to happen." Jett growls. I look at him and for some reason, I believe him. I take his hand and interlace my fingers into it. Surprising both of us with the gesture.

"How have you been able to replenish your magic without going unnoticed?" Kai asks, knowing that blood elves need blood, unlike humans who just need to rest.

"Master Runk and my three ladies got me the extra blood when needed. All four were sworn by oath to my father to keep my secret." I tell them. Jett begins to trace calming circles around the back of my hand.

"Where is your Master?" Enzo asks. My tears well but I bite back the pain.

"Dead." I swallow hard. "He died during an assassination attempt on my life."

I hear a feral growl rumble low in Jett's throat. "I'm sorry, it sounds like you were close." Kai states and I rest my head on his shoulder.

"You should turn me in. I am only going to bring you death and pain." I tell them, sounding defeated.

"Not going to happen. Is it?" Jett growls to the rest of them and they all nod. My heart pounds in my chest and I sit up, my head begins to pound again only this time it's so painful it brings me to my knees. "You need blood. Take it."

"I can't!" I scream but the pain is too much. I feel a grip on the back of my hair, wrenching my head back. Jett's wrists are in front of my mouth. He brings us both to our feet. The back of his knees pressing into the couch.

"Don't make me force you, Red. Drink." My fangs tingle and the scent of his intoxicating blood is too much. In one movement my fangs pierce his wrist and I greedily begin to consume his blood. "There, was that so fucking hard?"

I fall into him, forcing him backwards until he is seated, and I am straddling him.

It's like a breath of fresh air with a mix of ice hitting my veins. I drink and drink, a moan escaping me. Jett groans and his cock hardens beneath me.

"Fuck Red." I drink until the pain in my head fades. I release his wrist and then look at him. His hands find their way to my hips. "Red."

"Jett," I whisper, then look at his lips before I realize we are not alone here. Looking around I see the other three with lust in their eyes. Getting to my feet, I head to the base of the stairs before turning to look at them. "Thank you."

"Rest up, Ria." Kai states with a smile and for a moment I let my eyes wander, and I find myself catching them all adjusting their groins. Turning on my heel I run to my room, shut the door, and slide to the floor.

"What the fuck was that?" I run my tongue along my lips, shuttering with the flavor of Jett's blood. My sex is throbbing with need, and I feel myself flushed. "We can't go there, Ria. He was just saving you with his blood."

Still, I have never drank from the vein before. That was epic. I do not know how to describe it. This is unfamiliar territory for me, and I do not know how to feel about it. All the while I still have not told them my deepest and most sacred secret of all. Instinctively, I touch the jeweled headband and sigh. Relishing the familiarity of it.

"What do you think King Sarrs is doing right now?" I ask for my necklace. "You think he is going crazy searching for me? I hope not. I don't think I could face him." Getting to my feet, I make my way to my bed and lie down. The exhaustion of the day weighing on me as I drift off.

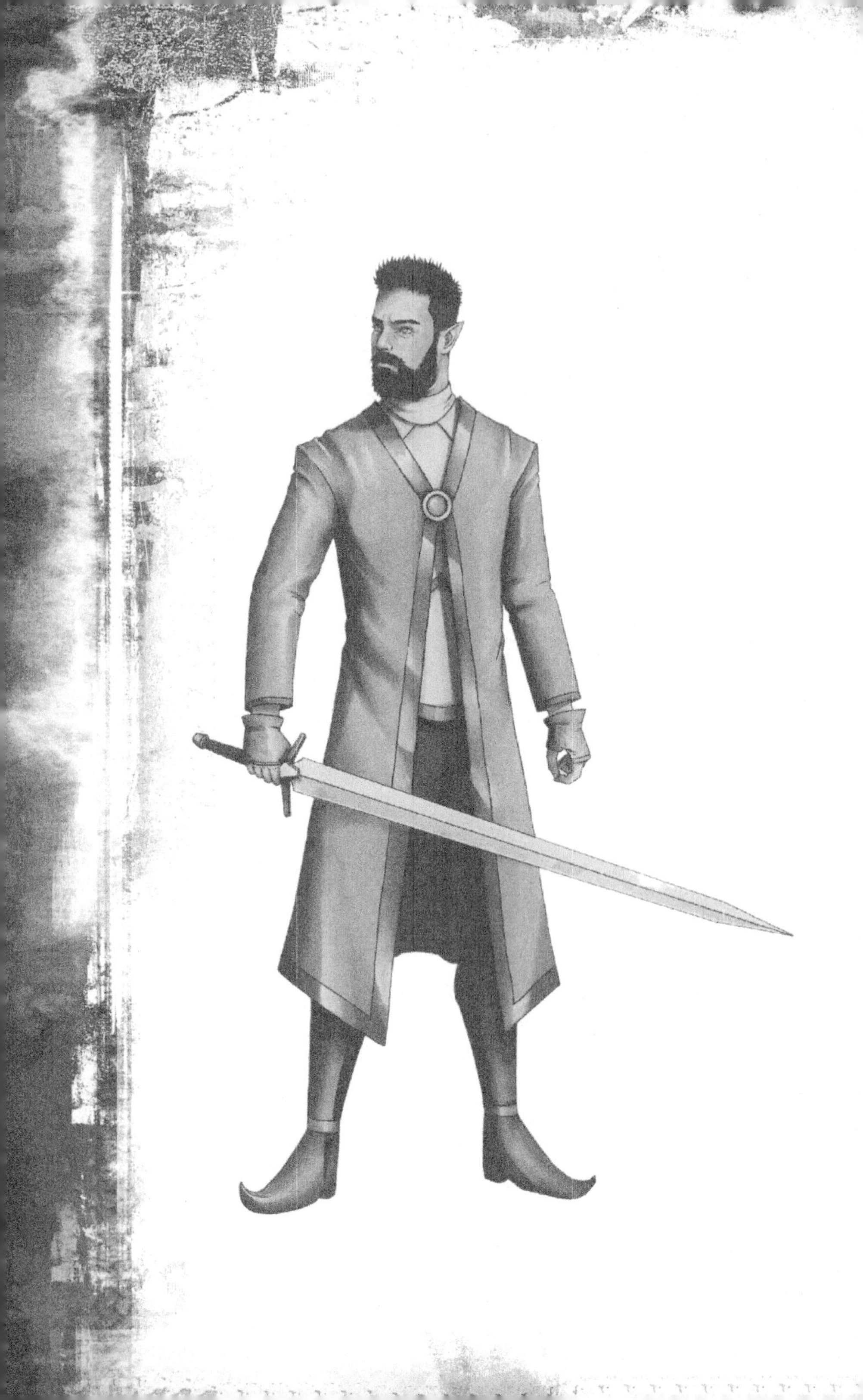

Chapter Eight

JETT

I watch as Red's door closes, and I instantly adjust myself, so the others do not see what she just did to me. Holy fuck that was sexy. If we were alone, I would have torn her clothes off and fucked her on this couch.

"What do we do about her?" Xander asks and I snap my gaze to him, baring my teeth.

"What do you mean? We fucking protect her. Keep her from him. Just like we were ordered too." I tell him.

"He didn't tell us what she was." Xander says walking towards me. I should not attempt to anger a mage, but for him I make an exception. "Why did you make her drink from you?"

"She needed blood." I tell him with a shrug.

"Bullshit. You saw her and fucking laid claim. You know what happens when we drink from another." Xander is in my face, and I am one second away from snapping his neck.

"What happens?" Kai asks. I step back from Xander. Humans know some things, but they do not know much about our laws and the magic of blood sharing.

"A blood bond forms between the two." Xander answers.

"Which means?" Enzo asks.

"It's like a mating bond." Xander answers, and I cannot help but smirk.

"You bastard." Kai charges at me, pushing me against the wall.

"You are all just pissed that I laid my claim before you got a chance." I growl.

"She is my fucking Fiancée, idiot." Kai growls. "She is mine."

"Not according to her. Plus, I don't see a fucking ring on her finger." I growl.

"He didn't complete the bond, Kai. Put him down. If he does not drink from her at the same time she drinks from him, the ritual isn't completed." Xander explains and I smirk.

"I mean do you blame me? Don't get mad at me for making a move you three are too pussy to take." I growl at them.

"I don't want her." Xander growls.

"Bullshit. Tell me something, Xander. Does your heart pick up when you catch her scent? When you saw her drink from me, didn't you want to tear me from her and feel her mouth on you?" I corner him. I do not like liars.

"Thought so." I state when he does not answer.

"Look, none of us have a right to claim her. She is not a piece of meat. She has been through trauma, and we need to be careful with her. The boss will not pay us if we do not bring her to him. Once the blizzard moves, we move." Enzo states and I nod. "Get some rest boys. And try not to kill each other."

"Won't make any promises." I growl shooting a glare at Xander. Blood elves are highly territorial. Which means if we see something we want, we take it and fight anyone for it. Red is something I want, and I will have her before any of these assholes do.

When they all go into their rooms I slip past their doors and make my way to hers, thinking about knocking but I find myself pressing my ear to it instead. Her soft breaths tell me she is asleep.

My heart pounds as her scent hits me. A mixture of fire and ice, earth and air, pain, and desire. Fucking hell what happened to you, Red? I hear her beginning to whimper and without thinking, I move inside. Closing and locking the door then she begins to thrash around. I move to the bed, draping my arm around her waist pulling her flush against my chest.

"It's okay, Red. You're safe." I say to her, running my fingers through her hair. I love the silky texture of it, the floral scent of her. My fingers catch on her tiara, and I wonder if she forgot to take it off. Gently, I grip it and begin to move it.

"Stop." She yells and then blasts me backwards with her magic. "What are you doing?" Her eyes are wide with fear, and I get to my feet rubbing the back of my head.

"Easy, Red. You were having a nightmare, so I came in here to try and calm you down."

"You touched my headband." She exclaims and I give her a look of incredulity.

"I was trying to remove it. Thought you forgot about it when you fell asleep." She straightens up and then crosses her arms across her chest, unintentionally pushing her breasts up. I try not to let my gaze wander, but I just can't help it.

"Oh, well don't touch it."

"Okay." We stand there for a moment, caught in an awkward silence. I wonder if she wants to drink from me again. I step forward at the same time she does. Soon there is no distance but a breath between us.

"Thank you, for earlier. I didn't know I needed to drink that badly." She looks up at me and I cannot help but want to kiss her. I need to know what it will feel like. Without any further hesitation, I press my lips to hers and pause for a moment. Thinking she will slap me until she kisses me back. Wrapping her arms around my neck.

My tongue presses against her lips asking for permission and she opens to me. Our tongues dance and I lift her up, she wraps her legs around my waist. I press her into the wall, showing just how badly I want her as my erection digs into her groin. My lips trail her jawline, to her earlobe, down her neck. A moan escaped her and then I kissed her again. I find the edge of her tunic, slipping my hand under it, and touching her heated skin.

I break our kiss and look at her, waiting for her to tell me to stop. She grabs my hand and moves it to her right breast. I palm it and run my thumb over the peek making her head tip back. I take advantage and kiss her neck, trailing my mouth up to her ear.

"Are you wet for me, Red?" I whisper huskily.

"Yes," she lets out a breathy moan.

"I want to feel you." I told her. "Can I feel you?"

"Yes," She moans again, and I crush my lips to hers as my hand goes from her breast down to the edge of her waistband.

"Ria," we immediately freeze the moment Kai's voice comes from the other side of the door. "Are you okay? I heard noises."

"Shit." She curses and I smirk at her. "Don't you dare. "She whispers.

"Shall I tell him to go away?" I whisper in her ear, kissing the sweet spot under it.

"No. Just let me talk to him." I nod and let her back down. I kiss her hard once more and then she walks away. Adjusting her hair. "I'm coming in." Kai states and then tries the handle.

"I'm coming." You will be. "Hey Kai, what's up?"

"Are you okay?" he asks.

"Yes, just dreaming. Are you okay?" He doesn't respond, all of a sudden, I hear a growl as the door is forced open and he is pushing me against the wall. His hand around my throat. I cannot help but laugh. "Kai, what the fuck are you doing?" She asks.

"His scent is all over you. You just had to do it. What the fuck are you doing to her?" Kai growls at me.

"Well, I would've been doing a lot more if you wouldn't have interrupted us." I told him.

"Did he force you?" Now that is insulting.

"What? No, I wanted him to." She answers.

"That's right, she wanted me to." I emphasize the me part. I see the hurt cross his face before he lets me go.

"Do you want him?" Kai asks her.

"No." she says, my eyes snapping to her. "I mean I don't know. Just leave, please both of you. I need some space." She answers.

"Come on, Red." I try to reach for her, but she steps away.

"What's wrong?" Enzo asks, stepping into the doorframe. Then I hear it, her increased heart rate, her breathing begins to quicken. Another panic attack.

"Move." I growl and then reach for her but there is a shield around her. "Calm down, Red. You are not in danger. Breathe."

"She's starting to panic, fuck what did you do?" Kai growls, but I ignore him because this is not about me. It is about her.

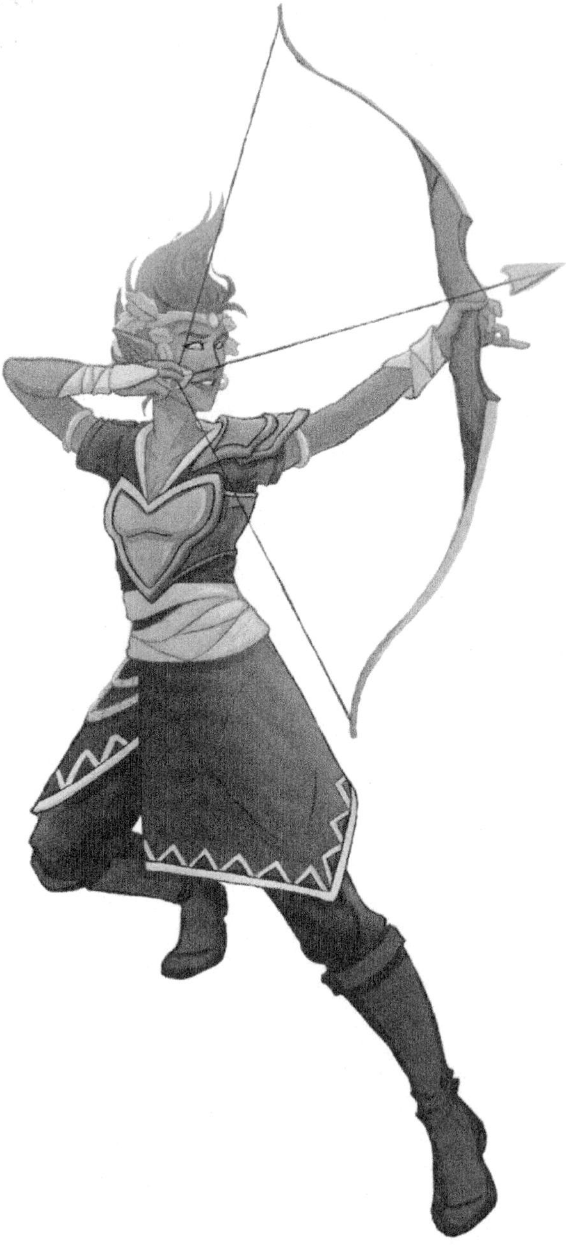

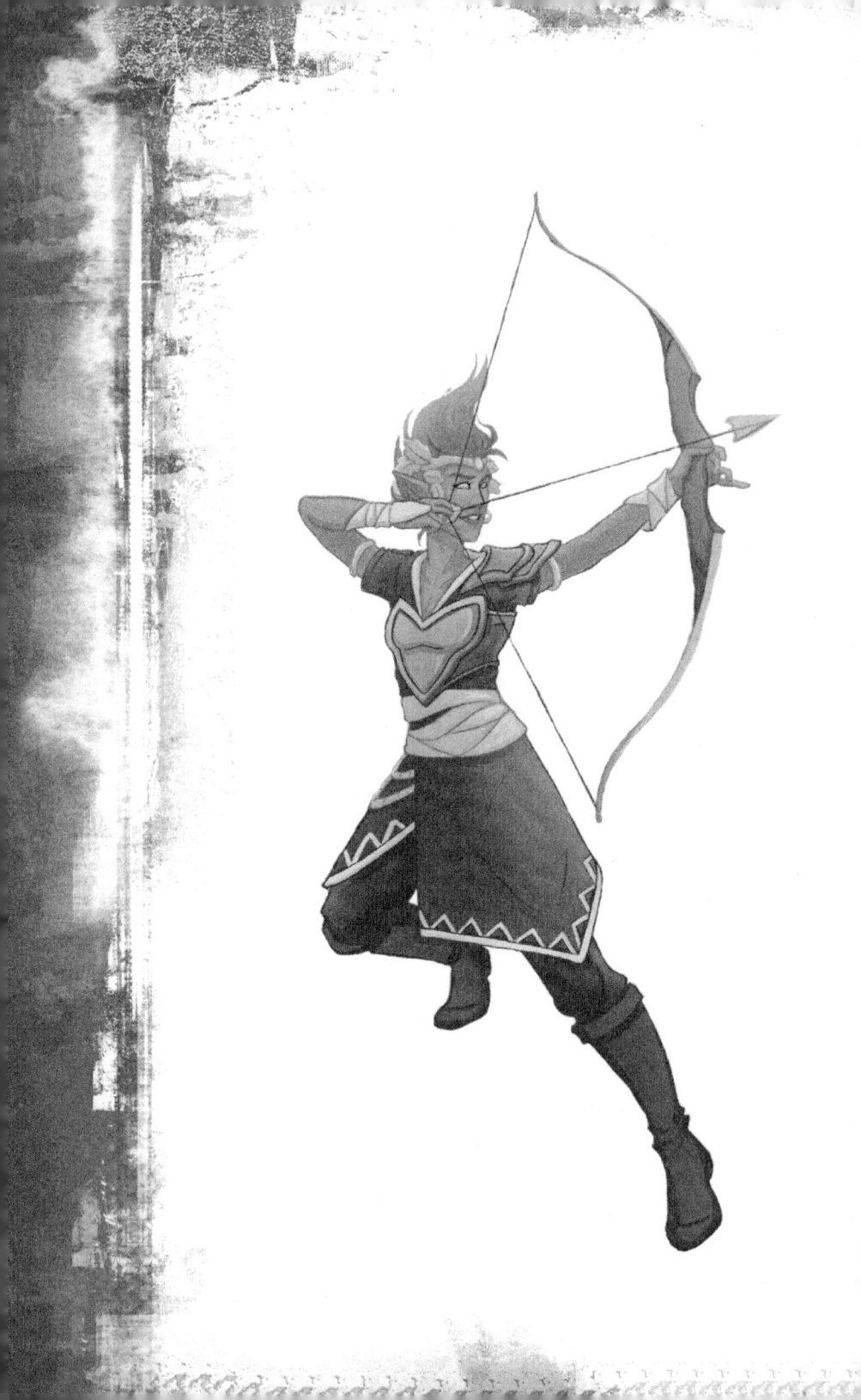

Chapter Nine

RIALYNNE

It is too much. All of them here surrounded me and then the way Jett made me feel before Kai came in. Goddess now he feels betrayed because I am his fiancée, but I found myself in the arms of another. I know they are trying to calm me down, but I cannot. The look on Kai's face, it's too much. I need to leave.

My bones begin to crunch, green scales start to overtake my skin as my face elongates into a dragon and I feel my wings burst from my back, breaking through the roof. Once I am completely morphed, I take flight. The blizzard is gone, the air is clear, I fly until I breach the cloud bank, the sky clear and calm.

I have not been able to transform in a while. Typically, I would need to wait until I knew all the ladies at the Cathedral were asleep. Sneaking out was not difficult when they did not think I would do anything as reckless as transfigure my body into an animal. Another skill Master Runk taught me how to control.

"Focus on this image, then envision yourself as the beast." Master Runk states as I run my hand over the glistening scales depicted. Dragons have been extinct since before the genocide of the druids. I want to be a dragon. "Good. Now jump."

Looking down at the castle grounds, I close my eyes, breathe in the cool night air, spread my arms, and step forward.

"Rialynne," Xander's voice cuts through my memory. Looking around, I do not understand how he would be up here. No one can fly except animals and air elementals. "Rialynne, you need to change back right now before someone sees you."

Standing on a moving tower of earth is Xander. I growl in protest. "Don't make me come get you."

I fly faster, banking in a zigzag motion to try and avoid him. "Come back Red." Jett's voice cuts through the rush of the clouds.

"We are just trying to protect you, Ria." Kai states.

"Please, my Queen." Enzo's voice cuts in next. Floating in the air, looking around, I see all four males surrounding me. Expecting to see anger on their different faces, but all I see is concern and fear. They fear me. No, they fear for me. For my safety. Xander on his tower of earth. Jett and his own cloud of air. Enzo and his fire tornado and lastly Kai, and his tower of snow.

"Please, Red. Let us help you." Jett's concern does something to my heart. The only people that have ever genuinely cared for me are Master Runk and my ladies. Slowly lowering myself to the ground, I transform back to my body. Using my fire magic to keep me warm as my clothes were destroyed when I transformed. Humiliation hits me as I cover my sensitive body parts, bringing my knees to my chest. The snow around me steams from the heat of my body.

"I've got you." Enzo's sweet voice comes from next to me. Covering me in his crimson tunic, he lifts me from the ground. Burying my face into his chest, our mixed fire magic fighting off the cold.

"I'm sorry." I whisper.

"You have nothing to be sorry for." He states. The walk back to the shelter is quicker than I expected. Kai has a pair of pants for me to put on while I button up Enzo's coat. When we are settled in our makeshift living room, I sigh, leaning my head on Kai's shoulder.

"Ria, we will not hurt you. Just tell us what is going on. How long have you had these powers and who trained you to use them? We may be kings, but you are our queen." Kai states. Looking around, I try to find doubt.

"You are a queen, Rialynne. But you are not my queen." Xander growls. "You realize how foolish that stunt was?" I do not know what to say.

"Back off." Jett growls and I swear I hear a growl coming from Kai too.

"No. Don't you three coddle her. She fucked up. Dragons have been long gone, if anyone had seen her, there would be an army here in a split second with questions we do not want to have to answer."

"I said back off." The two blood elves are now nose to nose. Growling at each other. "You aren't her mate. Stop acting like it." Xander growls back. I see a sinister smile form on Jett's face.

"Or what?" Jett instigates and my cheeks heat.

"Xander is right." All four look at me with shocked expressions. "I need to be more careful. Especially since we escaped an attack from the rebels. King Sarrs would not be happy to discover what I am."

I feel relieved as Jett backs off and leans up against one of the walls. Silence overtakes the room as if they are waiting for me to say more. Truth is, I am not sure what more I could say. Grabbing my necklace, I think of Master Runk again. *I wish you were here to guide me.*

"The blizzard has cleared. We need to get moving." Xander states.

"Where are we going to go?" I ask no one in particular.

"We, we will not be going anywhere. This little party is getting broken apart. As far as you individually, you need to go to the place where the rebels and Sarrs would not expect you to go." Xander states and I am starting to feel as though he is somehow in charge of the other three.

"Red's coming with me." Jett commands. Glaring at the other three, begging them to protest.

"You want her to stay here?" Enzo asks, answering a question I have been internally asking since we landed in this frozen tundra.

"I don't want her to do anything. There is no choice, she comes with me." Jett answers his cousin.

"Ria, you can choose." Kai tells me, and I know he wants me to come with him instead.

"No, she is coming with me. She has drunk from me, which means she will need my blood again." Jett smugly smiles. My mouth waters and my sex throbs at the memory of his blood flowing down my throat.

"Xander is a blood elf, she could always feed from him." Enzo states making Jett growl. He is going to rip these three apart if they try to take me from him. In a matter of seconds, they are all arguing. Xander is angry at them, suggesting I leave with him. He acts like I have some disease or something. Goddesses damn him for acting like that. I am a queen for Ares sake. This should be my choice and I know where I need to go.

"I am not going with any of you." I say in a whisper. They all snap their gazes back to me.

"What?" Jett asks.

"I said, I am not going with any of you. I have a place in mind. I know I will be safe and under the radar of the rebels and Sarrs." I tell them.

"Where?" Enzo asks.

"Klestria Academy." I answered him. I wait for them to protest but none of them do. "Since you are all quiet, I am going to assume you agree. Which would not matter anyways because I am queen. The queen of Klestria. I make my own decisions. I can enroll there under the guise as a student. Until it is safe for me to make my appearance at the palace again."

"It could work." Enzo states.

"It could do her some good. She needs more practice." Kai says.

"Just think of how hot she will look in those uniforms." Jett says with a wink making a blush rise in my cheeks. We all look to Xander, again making it seem as if his word is the final one.

"Fine. But we will go with you." I am the only one who protests as none of the others growl.

"Seriously? Why? I do not need you there. Who would be stupid enough to attack me while I am there? No one knows me." I speak.

"Everyone that was at the ball knows what you look like. You might be walking into a school full of entitled brats, but I am sure your image is plastered all over the place now. Which means you will need to glamorize your appearance." Xander says. Getting to my feet, I walk up to him. His earthy scent washes over me and my body reacts to it. Why does it do this with all four of them?

"You listen to me, Xander." I say bucking up to him. "I don't know what I did to make you hate me so much, but I am telling you right now that you are not in charge of me. I am a queen and in Klestria, that is my territory. I will no longer tolerate you and your bad attitude towards me." I growl.

"Back off, Faith." He growls as he peers down at me.

"Not until you tell me what I did to make you hate me so much." I growl back. "And my name is Rialynne. You don't get to call me anything other than that, Zain."

"You want to know what my problem with you is?" I nod and he takes a step closer to me, but I do not back down. "We don't know about you for years and then suddenly there is a queen in the fifth territory. Not only that, but one of us is forced to marry her. Then, we find out you are not just a queen. You're a fucking druid and an elite."

"Still don't see the problem." I start tapping my foot and I can see the anger in his eyes.

"Don't evaluate me, Faith. I won't hesitate to put you in your place." Mages are powerful. They accepted that spot when the druids died. Anyone who challenges them usually ends up dead, but he still does not scare me.

"I'm going to Klestria Academy without you because I can take care of myself. You may be a king, Zain, but you are not my king." I spit back his own words, then to add to the insult, turn my back on him. Which was a mistake as I am ripped back by my hair, straight into his chest.

Jett is there in a flash, his blade against Xander's throat. "Let her go."

"Not until she apologizes." He speaks. His breath kissed my ear, and I would think it would make me sick, but it does the opposite. What are you doing, Ria? You can get out of this. While he is distracted, I jam my elbow into his gut, knee his nose as he leans over, stomp on his foot, then knee his cock. Gripping his hair, I bare my teeth to him.

"I will never apologize to someone like you. I do not care who you are. You are unworthy of the title you wear. I am Rialynne Faith. The fucking queen of Klestria and I bow to no man." I let him go and then walked back to the center of the room.

"Damn, that's sexy as fuck." Jett states.

"You four will shut up and listen. I am doing this, and you will not follow me. If I find out that you have, I am going to do more than kick your ass. Got it?" I point at each of them. Xander is cupping his groin and for the first time I can see his scowl is gone.

"What about blood, Red? You are going to need it." Jett asks.

"I am sure they have it there." I answered him.

"If this is what you want." Kai says.

"We can't stop you." Enzo states.

"Fuck that." Jett starts.

"No, Jett. I need to do this, and you all need to get back to your own territories. I am sure while I am there, I can improve upon my skills until I am ready to take my place as queen again. That is something I need to do on my own." I tell them. "End of discussion. I am going to sleep. In the morning, Xander, I need you to take me there; if you would be so kind."

He nods and before they can say anymore, I turn and rush back up the stairs to my room. I do not know if I will sleep, but I do know that this is the right move. They will all come to understand.

After tossing and turning, I decide to get up and head to the bathroom. Relieving myself helps a lot. As I open the door, I am hit with the scent of air and snow.

"Jett," I whisper. In a flash I am tugged against a hard, bare chest and a door that is not to my room is closed and locked.

"Hey, Red." One of his arms wraps around my waist, as the other remains at his side.

"What are you doing?" I whisper again as I feel his lips trailing kisses down my neck. Instead of pushing him away, I move to give him better access.

"I am finishing what we started." He says in a teasing way before gripping my hips and turning me to face him.

"And what did we start?" I say with a smile. My heart is racing with anticipation as my stomach churns with anxiety.

"Do I need to remind you?" His hand moves to my cheek before he crashes his lips to mine in a possessive kiss. I moan as his tongue dances with mine. He hardens against my stomach as I run my hands down his chest. He picks me up and lays me down on his bed.

I open my legs as he kisses me deeper.

"Jett," I moan.

"Do you want me to stop?" he says pausing.

"No." I answer before reaching up to undo my tunic. He groans as I shrug it off, baring my breasts to him. His mouth clamps down on the right one causing me to arch my back as he sucks then bites me, piercing my skin and drinking from me. The rush of endorphins washes over me as he sucks my blood into him. "Jett, I…please…"

He lifts his mouth off me, licking the blood from his mouth before kissing me. I taste myself on his tongue, and it awakens a hunger in me. "Tell me what you want."

"I want you inside me." I tell him and he kisses me again before trailing kisses down my body. Gripping the sides of my pants, he pulls them off me until I am completely bare before him. I watch as he drops his own pants. A gasp leaves me as I look upon the girth of his cock. "Is this your first time, Red?" He asks, gripping the base and running his hand up his shaft.

"Yes." I answered him. He crawls towards me, pushing my legs to the side and trailing kisses up my inner thigh causing me to moan. "I'm going to show you what it means to be worshiped. You will come on my fingers, tongue, and cock. Do you understand me, Red?"

Goddess, those words and promises have me clenching and dripping with need.

"Answer me, Red."

"Yes."

"Good girl."

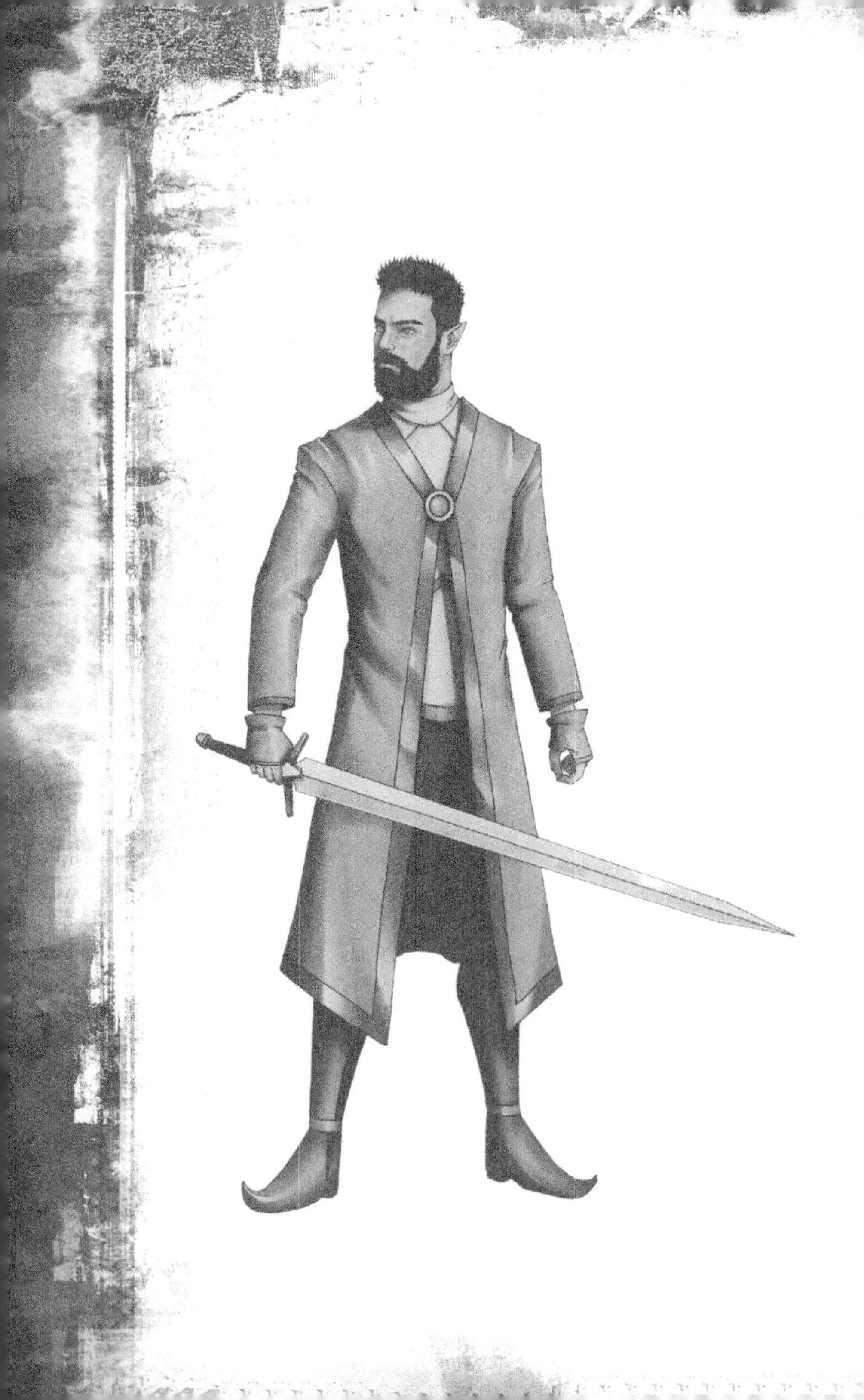

Chapter Ten

JETT

I run my tongue through her folds, using my left hand to hold her down. I flick my tongue across her clit before sucking it.

"Fuck, Jett." She moans encouraging me further. I insert one finger, feeling her dripping. She is so taut, and my cock is hard as steel with anticipation. I continue to fuck her with one finger, then two, as I lick and suck her clit. "Please."

I can tell by her hips bucking she is close. I insert a third finger and she practically screams my name. I lick up her juices, swallowing the sweet flavor of her. Crawling up to her, I kiss her so she can taste herself.

"Jett, I need you inside me." she says breathlessly.

"Since you asked so sweetly," I tease. Gripping my cock, I take the tip and swirl it around her sensitive clit. Her nails rake down my back. "It's going to hurt, but I will go slow."

"I'm ready." She says and I kiss her as I slowly start to enter.

"Fuck, you're tight. I might not last long." I growl and as I inch in, I wait until I am fully sheathed inside her before kissing her again.

"Are you okay?"

She nods but her eyes are closed.

"Look at me, Red." She opens her eyes.

"I'm good, don't stop." I kiss her again before I pull out and thrust in again. Picking up my rhythm as she becomes fully adjusted to me.

"You're going to cum two more times, Red." I promise her.

"Jett," she moans, and I move my hand between us, finding her clit and circle while I continue to plunge into her. "I'm close."

"Cum for me, Red." I kiss her as I pick up pace and when I feel her clench around me, I muffle her scream with my mouth. I pause so I do not cum myself. "Good girl."

"I don't know if I can manage it."

"Yes, you can. Do you want me to stop?"

"No, it feels amazing. Keep going."

"Thank fuck because I would've died if you said yes." She giggles and I pull out.

"On your hands and knees." I command and she does not even hesitate. I line myself up with her and thrust back in. Gripping her hips, I continue to fuck her, giving her what she needs. "Touch your clit, I want you to cum for me."

"Jett," she moans. I slap her ass and she gasps. "Now, Red." I watch as she begins to stimulate herself. I pull out and plunge three fingers in before pulling them out, thrusting my cock inside her again. "I'm going to fuck you here with my fingers, Red." I run my fingers over her tight hole, and she whimpers.

Pulling out, she growls in protest until I insert my fingers inside her pussy, with the intention of using her own cum as lube. When I feel them coated, I pull out and then thrust back in with my cock before inserting one finger, then two into her ass, she moans. I continue to fuck her with my cock and finger.

"You're so responsive, Red. Such a good girl, taking my cock and fingers." She clenches around me before pushing back to meet my pace.

"Jett, I'm so close." She breathlessly states. I insert another finger and she clenches around my fingers and cock, causing the last of my self-control to leave me as I fill her with my seed.

We fall forward.

"Fucking hell, Red." I say as I kiss her shoulder.

"Back at you." She speaks. That was the best sex I have ever fucking had. I pull out, get up, grab a towel, and then clean her up before cleaning myself. She scoots underneath the covers, and I pull her to my chest.

"Thank you."

"For what?" I ask.

"For giving me what I needed." She tells me.

"All you need to do is ask, Red. I'd do anything for you." She turns over and looks at me.

"Why? You hardly know me."

"Because you are mine and I take care of what is mine."

"We aren't blood bonded, Jett. You can't say that."

"Do I need to remind you who this pussy belongs to?" I ask while cupping it. She shakes her head and bites her lip. "Why'd you give yourself to me if you don't want to be mine?"

"Because the way I feel around you, is the same way I feel when I am around the rest of them." She admits and a surge of jealousy hits me. "I don't know why. Maybe there is something wrong with me." I tilt her head so she can look at me.

"There is nothing wrong with you, Red. I don't want to share with you, but as you said, we are not mates so I don't have the right to deny you the others if you chose to give yourself to them too." It hurts but I cannot force a blood bond on her. It is a choice she needs to make on her own.

"Do you think they heard us?" she asks, and I smile at the blush rising in her cheeks.

"I'd say so, but I don't think they were concerned because they probably heard you moaning in pleasure and not in pain." I tell her and she smiles.

"Jett,"

"Yeah Red?"

"If I do not see you after tonight, I want you to know I am happy I gave myself to you. You have set the bar extremely high for me in this department." I feel sad by the idea that this might be the last time I get to hold her like this. I want to get to know her. I know she is my mate, even if she does not know it. I feel it in my bones.

"I'm happy too, Red." She kisses me before her eyes drift close and soon she is fast asleep. "I will always be here for you, Red."

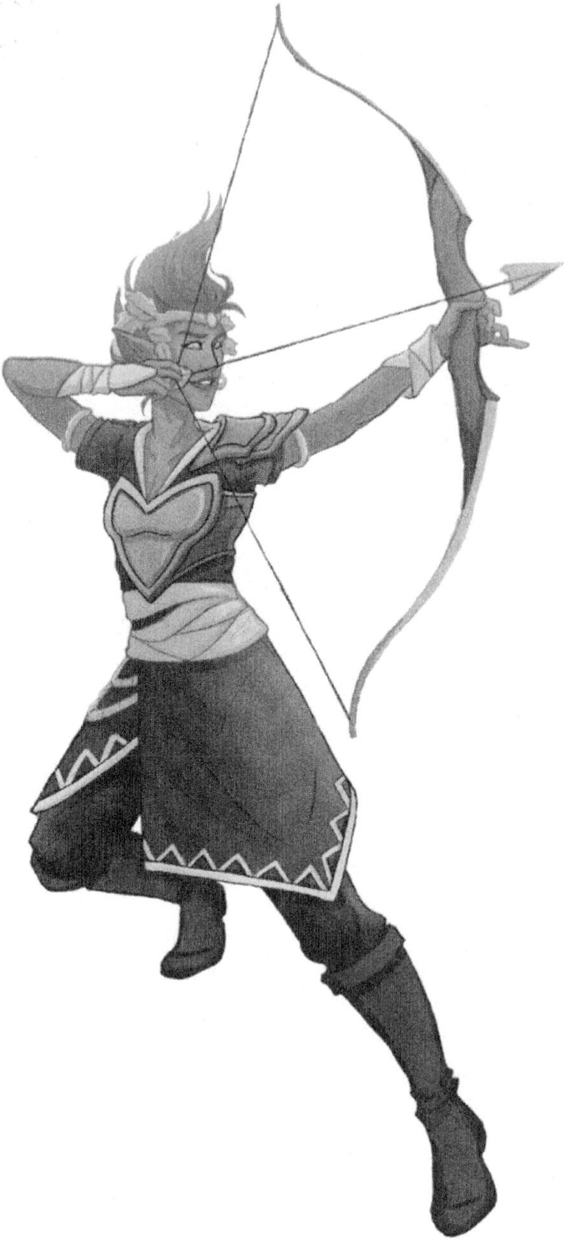

Chapter Eleven

RIALYNNE

I woke up with a bare male body behind me and something hard poking into my ass. Turning around, I see Jett smiling at me. He kisses me without warning before hovering over me. "Morning sex?"

"I don't know if I can manage it, I'm sore." I feel his tip touching me and any pain I was feeling is turned into pleasure, as I start dripping again. "On second thought…"

I pull him on me and kiss him, arching into him as he thrusts inside me. "I'm going to make you scream so that they know just who this pussy belongs to."

His dirty words add to my need as I dig my heels into his ass. I feel my climax building as he circled my clit with his finger.

"Cum for me. Tell them whose cock is giving you pleasure."

"Jett," I scream and then he kisses me hard as I climax on him. He pulls out and before I catch my breath, he flips me over and thrusts back inside me. Palming my breasts and kissing my neck before sinking his teeth into me. The feel of his cock, teeth, and finger are sending me over the edge again as I scream his name.

"Good girl." He praises and I fucking enjoy that. "Tell me what you want."

"I want you in my mouth. I need to taste you."

"Fuck, Red. You're so perfect." He pulls out of me and then lays on the bed. I crawl up to his cock, gripping the base, I swirl my tongue around the tip, tasting the beaded cream at the top, before taking him completely to the back of my throat and swallowing.

I run my tongue along the shaft before keeping a bobbing motion and he threads his fingers in my hair, above my headband. Any anxiety I had about him touching it has vanished, since he has not tried to take it off since the first time. I dig my nails into his ass and urge him to fuck my mouth.

"You want me to fuck your pretty mouth?" I moan in response, and he picks up a rhythm. I choke and gag and then he thrusts once more before spurting his hot cum into my throat which I swallow. He pulls out and kisses me hard tasting himself. "So perfect." He wipes my mouth before pulling me into his embrace.

"I wish we could stay here." I confess, not meaning to.

"Me too, Red." He says before we pull away from each other.

"I guess we should get showered and changed. We are going to have to face them eventually."

"I will kill them all if you want me to." He smiles, making me laugh.

"No. We are consenting adults." I tell him and he kisses me once more before we make our way out of his room and straight into the bathroom. Once we are showered and clean, the smell of cooked bacon floods my senses. There is something I need more than food.

"Good morning," Jett says as we take seats on the sofa. I try to get a read on the room, and it seems very awkward.

"Jett and I had sex." I say, and they all look at me. "Don't dwell on it." I bite into my bacon, but my gaze keeps landing on each of their pulsing veins. The blood of them calling to me.

"So, you have made your choice then?" Kai asks, sounding pained. Putting my plate down, I get up and make my way over to where he is seated. Straddling him, I cup his face and kiss him. Soaking in the seafoam scent of him.

"No. I'm not choosing." I say. I get up and move to Enzo who pulls me into a crushing kiss full of fire and smoke. I move to Xander next, looking at him. He does not move as I stand on my tiptoes and place a soft kiss on his lips. I back up but I am soon crushed against him in a claiming kiss. His tongue mingles with mine making my sex throb again.

"Good." He speaks.

"Xander, I need blood and since I drank from Jett, I want to drink from you too." I confess. His eyes move side to side, like he is assessing me. He moves his wrists up to my mouth and I bite into it.

Moaning against the pure power I feel draining from him into me. I hear Jett curse, but I do not care.

I pull back and lick my lips. "Thanks."

Someone clears their throat and I turn around, looking at all four kings. I know this will be the last time I see them for a while. The rest of breakfast goes by without incident. They all make small talk about plans while I try to wrap my head around the fact that I will be in my own territory under the guise of a student attending our academy.

"Ready to go?" Kai asks, snapping me out of my stupor.

"Yes." I say with a smile. They form a circle around me, and I kiss each of them once more. "Thank you for saving me. One day, I hope we will all rule in unity."

Xander opens the portal and I step through; instant regret takes over me as the four of them disappear. I land in sand right outside the large iron gates that lead into the school. A large shielded crest with the 'K' symbol stares back at me.

Now or never, Ria. I clutch my necklace and step up to the gate.

It opens and I walk inside, heading straight to the large building at the center that reminds me of the Cathedral.

Shoulders bump into me as many students dressed in various uniforms pass by me. I find myself standing at the center of a circle lobby that has four corridors shooting off it.

"You must be new." A female's voice comes from behind me. Turning I see a brunette human with a quiver full of arrows and a bow strapped across her body. She is so tall I must crane my neck to look at her face.

"What makes you say that?" I ask.

"You are acting lost." She speaks. "I'm a hunter, I can see a stray from a mile away."

"Right. I need to find the Dean's Office." I told her.

"I can take you." She smiles at me, and I follow her straight ahead, through the crowd of students until we are standing outside a glass door with the label Office of Admissions painted on it. As I push through it, I am instantly greeted with the smell of cinnamon. There is a single mahogany desk with a human sitting behind it.

"Miss Faith?" She asks not even looking up.

"Yes, Ma'am." I answer.

"Here is your school handbook, class books, schedule of classes, and house key. You will find your room is already stocked with your uniforms. Since you claimed fire as your element, you will have all your classes in that training hall. Don't break any of the rules. If you do, expulsion means a meeting with King Sarrs, and he decides whether you go to prison or not." I gulp and make a mental note not to get expelled.

"Thank you."

"Here is your map, welcome to Klestria Academy." I look down at my stack and try to figure out which way I need to go to get to the Hunter House. After I decided I was coming here, Xander sent a message through a portal with all my information on it to the admissions office. I chose Hunter as my order because archery is my skill.

"Looks like you will be living in my house, named Antoinette." The girl from before reaches out a hand, I take it. "Follow me. Classes don't start for a week, so that gives you plenty of time to get settled in."

"Thank you, my name is Ria." No need to tell her my full name. My glamor seems to be holding up. I did not change much except my hair is shorter and my eyes are not as bright.

"That's a nice name. What's up with the gold piece?" she asks.

"My headband?" I ask, trying to play it off.

"Yeah, seems too fancy to just be a hair piece." She states. Hunters are notorious for their perceptive abilities. I am gonna need to watch this one.

"It was a gift from my Mother before she died." I blurt out.

"I'm sorry." She says and we fall silent as we walk out of the main building, down some steps following a sidewalk that seems to lead to a tall house with a black flag with a silver knocked arrow sewn into it.

As we walk up the steps to it, my arms feel like they might fall off my body if I do not set my pile of stuff down. The outside is made of thick tree logs and a steel roof. We enter through a single black door and a gust of fresh air hits me, cooling my skin.

A lounge area is directly passed the foyer. Three large leather couches all sit around a round table. A spiral staircase is just off to the side, and we make our way there.

"More stairs." I ask.

"Yep, you'll get used to it." I follow her up the three flights until we step off. There is a single row of five doors and mine is the very last one. Without asking, she takes my key and opens my door. A desk is to the left and I set my stack down. There is a single bed pushed to the back and across from that is an open-faced wardrobe with crimson uniforms.

"Where is the bathroom?" I ask.

"It is a co-ed one on the second floor." She answers and I am suddenly self-conscious because only one person has seen me naked, and that was Jett. My heart squeezes at the thought of him and I do not know why. "Don't worry, the males don't shower at the same time as us. If they do, we just kick them out."

"Okay." I let out a breath and it suddenly became awkward between us.

"I'll let you get settled, if you need me, I am the first door down the hall."

"Thank you." I say and she exits my room closing it. I fall back onto my bed and close my eyes. *I cannot believe I am at this school right now. What is wrong with me?* We are hiding from psycho rebels and the king. Who will kill us for who we are? Xander was right. Thinking of the boys, memories of their kisses flash through my mind and I feel as though a part of me is missing without them around me.

What is that about? My cheeks heat as memories of Jett and I flood through my mind, and I begin to think about the others. What would it be like to have them there too? My hands move on their own as I remember the way Jett touched me. A knock sounds and I snap up feeling like I got caught doing something wrong.

Opening the door, I see a raven-haired elf standing there with a crimson tunic on her. "Hi, my name is Melody. I am the Hunter house leader."

"Hi, I'm Ria." Without asking her to, she barges into my room and looks around.

"Wow, your own room, aren't you lucky? What cock did you suck to get this?" Her demeanor changed from friendly to bitchy in a split second.

"Excuse me?" She backs up to me any friendly nature of her dissolving.

"Listen to me, Ria. I am the head of this school. What I say goes." I cross my arms trying to figure out who she thinks she is talking to.

"I see what this is, you're trying to intimidate me. I am sorry, but that won't work with me. Not that it is not any of your business, I have not sucked any cocks to get this room. This is what the admin lady gave me." She scoffs as if she does not believe me.

"Do as I say, and we won't have problems. For starters, Enzo is off limits." Did she just say what I think she did? "Enzo? Who is that?" my heart begins to pound and it's almost so loud it's drowning her out.

"My boyfriend, that's who." Then it cannot be him. How funny is it that I hear about a second Enzo? "Anyways, we need to head down. It's the first night assembly."

"Right." I grab my key and map, before following her out and locking the door. Antoinette meets me at the stairs, grabbing me by the arm, more than likely to save me from Mouthy Melody.

"You, okay?" she asks as we make our way down the path to Training North.

"Yeah, just got accused of sucking cock by Melody." I tell her, and she laughs at my bluntness.

"She is just jealous. Her first year here she had two roommates. You really are lucky to have gotten that room. But seeing as you are the last person to fill, it was meant to be." She winks at me, and I realize I am starting to like this human.

The hall is packed with students all in their designated uniforms. Earths in green, Fire in red, Water in blue, and Air in gold.

"I am a water elemental so I will have to sit with them, but we can meet after if you'd like?" she asks, and the gleam in her eye tells me she wants me to say yes.

"Okay, I am on fire." She smiles at me, and we break apart. I find my seat at the very back, closest to the exit so if I need a quick getaway, I can use it. The hall quiets down, and a tall human with white short-cut hair and a white mustache, steps forward.

"Good evening students, for those that do not know who I am, my name is Dean Ziba. There are a few announcements that need to be addressed. Firstly, welcome first year students. Klestria Academy is the most prestigious academy in Zavinia and only the finest students are accepted. Be that as it may, your position at this school is not set in stone. You will each be graded on your academics and performance by your professors. I will receive a monthly report. If you fall behind on individual points, you will be expelled."

That is discouraging to say the least. Some of my fellow students would agree since there is a vast amount of 'gasp' and 'awes' from the crowd.

There will be Irfu tryouts in two days. But I will let the coach explain that to you. This year we will have four guests of honors filling in teaching positions for each elemental combat class as well as your other classes."

"I wonder who it is." Some girls with pink hair whispered to no one in particular.

"It's the four kings." I snap my head to a red-haired boy sitting in front of her.

"No way. Why would the four kings take teaching jobs here?" a pink-haired girl asks. She is right. There is no way the four males I spent the last couple days with are here. Especially when I told them not to come here.

"I would like for you all to give a warm and honorable welcome to your four new professors." Just like that, all four of their scents hit me without warning.

"King's Kai, Enzo, Xander, and Jett." My world slows as everyone around me bends the knee. I am left standing looking like a disrespectful idiot because these idiots decided to come here after all.

"Problem, Red?" Jett asks with a raised brow. I swallow then bend my knee.

"You may rise." Xander says in his kingly voice. This is bad. Not just bad, but really fucking bad. Why would they come here? Why would they teach here? What about their people? And King Sarrs? I narrow my eyes at all four of them as the room gets to their feet.

"Irfu tryouts will be tough. Each House will have a team of ten, including a captain. Just because you have been on those teams previously, does not mean you will make the cut this year." Jett explains to the crowd of students.

"They are hot." The pink-haired girl exclaims.

"Dude, they are off limits. For starters, they are kings and now our teachers. That goes against the number one rule in the handbook." The red-haired boy tells her.

"Doesn't matter. They're royalty. I am sure the normal rules do not apply to them. Besides, King Enzo and I are already dating." Mouthy fucking Melody did not just say that did she? Snapping my head to her, I growl.

"There is no fucking way a king would ever date you." It poured out of my mouth before I could stop it.

"Shut it trailer scum. Don't be jealous if a king chose me and not you." She bares her teeth at me. I curl my fists, my power edging my skin just to be released. *Calm down, Ria. Remember we are supposed to be in hiding.* Thinking ignoring her is the best way to avoid conflict, I turn and head out the room.

"Hey, you, okay?" I turned around and noticed the red-haired boy followed me out. He is a human with blue eyes and dark skin.

"Yeah, I just needed some air. It's kind of intense there." I told him. He rubs the back of his neck before speaking.

"I'm Damarias Castro, it's my first year here too." He reaches out his hand. I take it.

"Ria Faith, nice to meet you." I smile and we break contact. It would not be a completely daft idea to make friends while I am here.

"I'm a mage. What about you?" he asks, trying to keep the conversation flowing.

"Hunter."

"That's cool. Where are you familiar?" my mind blanks out at his question. Something I have not thought of. *Think, Ria, think.* Out of nowhere, I conjured up a small green dragon. It curls its tail around my neck and nuzzles its tiny head against my ear. His blue eyes widened with shock and awe. "A dragon? That's amazing."

"Yeah, I have always wanted to meet one, but since that is impossible, I just imagine that is what my familiar would be if they were still around. My Uncle used to read me the stories about them."

"The Time of Dragons & Druids?" he asks, and I smile.

"You know that book too?"

"I love that book! Imagine if they were both still around today. Maybe the shadow rebels wouldn't be an issue anymore." A memory of the noise they made floats in my mind causing me to shiver. "Are you cold?"

"No." An awkward silence develops but it's soon broken with the outpour of students.

"Hey, Ria, where'd you go?" Antoinette asks as she walks up to me.

"Just out here."

"Hey Damarias," she blushes.

"Hey Toni."

"Do you two know each other?" I look between them, sensing some type of familiarity.

"Yeah, we both grew up in Fortunia Village in the Oceaniansphere." Antoinette answers.

"That's great." I say, too eagerly.

"Are you hungry?" Damarias asks. I am not hungry for food; I am aching for a chance to chew four assholes out.

"I'm good, you two should head out. I will meet you back at the house." I tell them all in line. "See you later." Antoinette smiles as they start walking towards the Chow Hall, which looks like it is in the opposite direction of Training North. I watch as the last of the students disperse in various directions before slipping back inside. Peeking around the raised stone steps, I eye the four kings at the center, speaking in hushed tones.

"You can come out, Red."

Damn it Jett.

Coming out from my not so discreet hiding spot, I stomp towards them.

"How dare you!" I almost scream as I walk up the five steps leading to the raised platform. They all move in front of me, standing, crossed arm, as one unit. These are the four most powerful elementals in all of

Zavinia. If I were smart, I would be intimidated by them, but I know they will not hurt me. Not because they cannot, but because I am more powerful than all of them, and they know it.

"We didn't follow you here." Xander says with a shrug.

"Not as students." I scoff.

"You never said anything about professors." Enzo comments.

"Are you serious right now? I cannot believe how idiotic you four are being. Sarrs knows you are here; I am assuming since you were introduced as the four fucking kings. Now he suspects I am here. To include the damn shadow rebels and their mysterious leader. Did that even cross your mind?" My hands are on my hips and my chest is tight with the rage I feel.

"Ria, let us explain, but not here." Kai's gentle tone tries to ease my anger, but I will not fall for it.

"No." I turn on my heel, but I am stopped by a firm grip on my arm pulling back against a hard chest. Jett's scent washes over me. One hand is wrapped around my waist while the other is gripping my forearm. I feel his mouth near my ear.

"I've missed you, Red. We will explain this, and you will listen, or I will have you tied to my bed choking on my cock until you beg me for release." His threats should piss me off, but my traitorous body has other ideas.

"Okay."

"Good girl." He says before nipping my ear and letting me go.

"Meet us here." Jett slips a piece of paper in my hand before they all turn to leave me standing there, trying to catch my breath and figure out what the hell just happened to me.

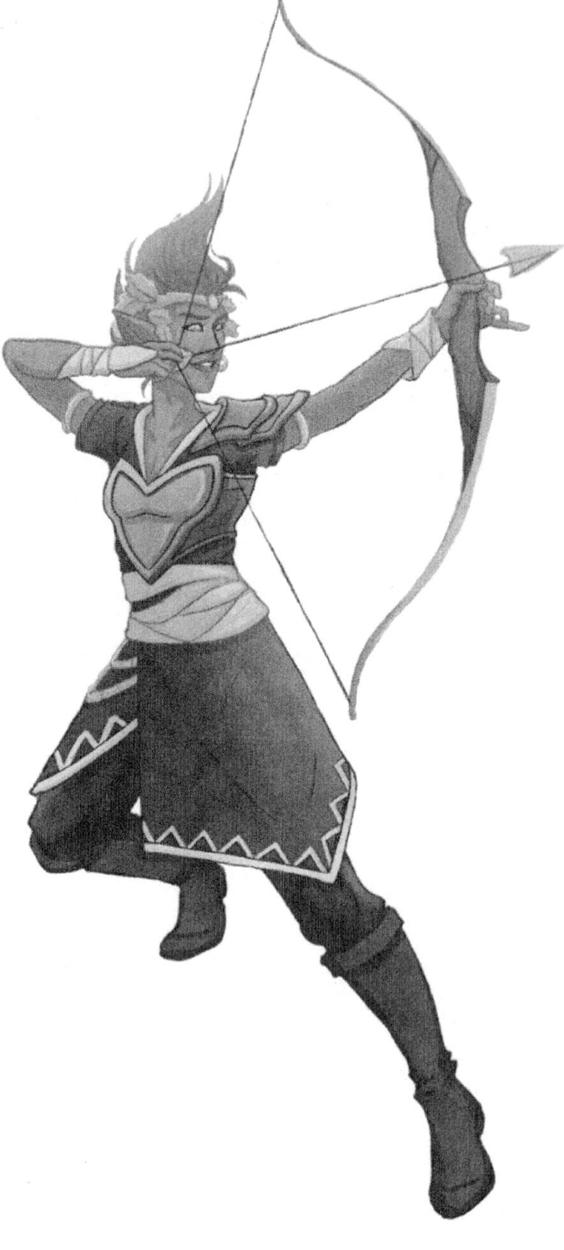

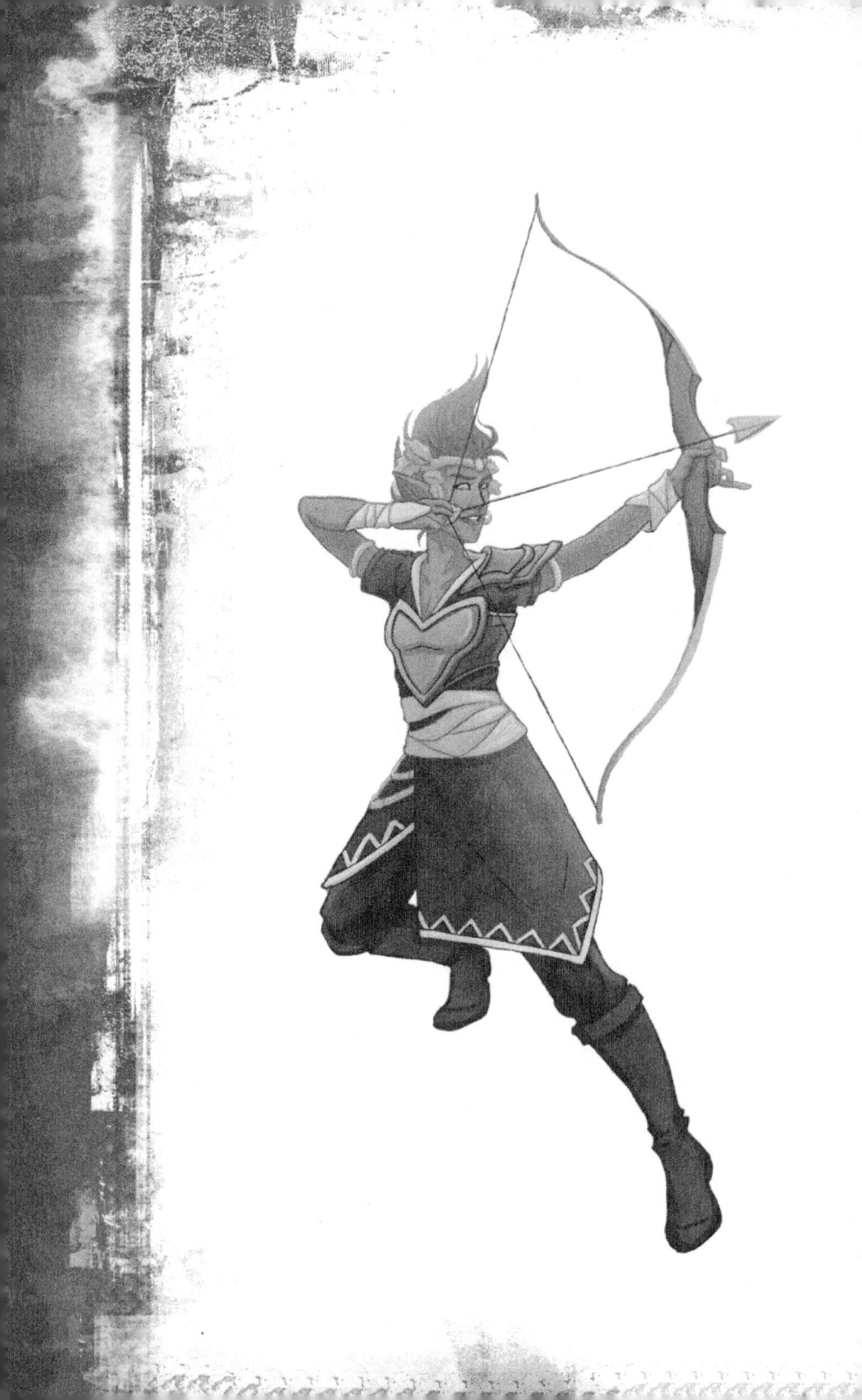

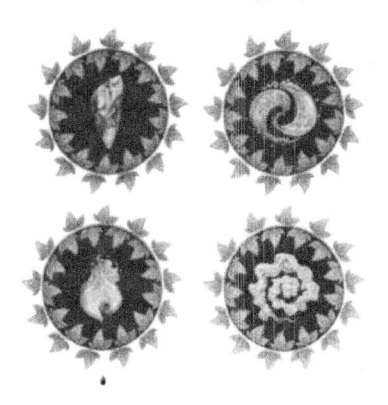

Chapter Twelve

RIALYNNE

Looking down at the paper he slipped in my hand, I found the words *Library, history section, now Red. Or else.* I can practically hear Jett's demanding tone, feel him all over my body.

"Pull yourself together. You are a queen." I whisper to myself before pulling out my map. I am on the backside of Training North and the library is just to the east. Putting the paper back in my pocket, I head towards the pathway that connects the buildings.

From the outside, the building looks well kept. Its rusted colors of the bricks compliment the environment of Klestria. Its' windows are spread out every few feet with misted glass and a large double wooden door sits in the center of four white columns, connecting it to an awning casting shade over the stone steps.

I pull on the iron handle and I am immediately greeted by the smell of parchments. Bookshelves line both sides starting from the front and continuing straight to the back. At least fifteen on either side. At the center is a round desk with two workers, typing away on their computers, not even granting me so much as a glance.

I make my way past them, walking until I come upon the history section at the back right.

I get the urge to run my fingers along the spines as I walk down the aisle, admiring all the unread knowledge these books hold. My hand immediately stops on a black spine. Turning, I pull it out, run my hand over the vacant cover before opening it and smelling the pages. Every bookworm loves the smell of books. Or at least that is what Mother would tell me whenever she brought a new one in to read.

"Jada, the last Elite Druid. A lesson in history and power." I whisper as I read the title page. "Who wrote this?"

"There is no known scholar." An older gentle voice comes from beside me. Looking I see it's one of the Librarians. She has snow-white hair tied back in a bun revealing her sharped ears. *I have never seen a blood elf appear this old.*

"Did you know this druid?" I ask, trying to get a sense of her age. She gives me a closed mouth smile.

"Indeed, I did. Jada was a student here when the academy first opened."

"And when was that?"

"Eight centuries give or take a few years." Goddess, she must be, "I am nine hundred and one if that's what you are wondering. Not that I plan on joining Ares any time soon. My father lived to be almost fifteen hundred."

"Oh." Is the only word in my entire vernacular that seems to pop out.

"If you need anything, dear, just ask. That is what I am here for."

"Thank you," I paused to get her name.

"You may call me Madame Serafena." She winks at me, her purple iris twinkling, before turning back to her cart of books, continuing to place them back on their shelves.

"I'm Ria, by the way." She waves a hand at me before starting to hum to herself. Looking back, I turn to the first page and begin to read, only to find it's written in a completely different language.

"What?" I say, too loud to be considered a whisper. Looking around, I try to find Madam Serafena, but she is already gone. I feel a tingle of magic touching my fingers and before long I am pulled from where I was standing into a different room. Looking around, I see three couches lined around a stone fireplace and four males staring back at me.

"Hello, Rialynne." Xander says with a smirk.

"Where am I?" I ask while looking around.

"Our own secret spot within the walls of the academy. Can't be seen meeting with a student. It would send the wrong message." Enzo answers.

"What you got there, Red?" Jett says as he reaches for my book. I snap it back, baring my teeth. "You want to play?" He charges for me, capturing my jaw in his right hand before pressing his lips to mine. I cannot help the moan that leaves my lips at the feel of him. Some sense of control comes back to me, and I push him off using my air magic. The bastard laughs.

"I'm still pissed at all of you. How dare you come here? To the place that is meant for me to feel safe."

"Ria, we came here to keep you safe." Kai answers.

"How are you being here keeping me safe? Don't Sarrs think I am with one of you?" They exchange glances with each other, seeming to have a silent conversation. "He doesn't know I went with you? Where does he think I am?"

"We had to produce something he would believe in. A small lie to keep him off your scent and something that will send word to the shadow rebel leaders' ears." Enzo answers.

"What?" I ask, trying to get them to cut to the chase.

"You're dead." Xander answers with a stoic face. I slump down on the couch, placing the book on my lap before trying to figure what this means.

"No one will search for a ghost." Jett says.

"But then that means Sarrs will continue to rule Zavinia and Klestria. I have been gone a day; how did you kill me in all that time? Didn't you all go back to your territories?"

"Time works differently within the walls of this academy. A day to you is a month on the outside." Kai answers. That explains why Jett acted like he had not seen me in forever.

"Mages don't have that kind of magic."

"No, but druids do." Xander states. "It was the first druid that founded this academy." His comment made me think of Jada.

"Okay, so I'm dead. What now? What happens when I am ready to leave here and reclaim my throne?" I ask them.

"Then we will stand by your side." Kai says.

"Speak for yourself." Xander snorts.

"It would be wiser if you were already married to one of us when that day comes. In the meantime, we recommend you master all your powers and get to know us. Then, we have all agreed that whomever you choose, we will all continue to support you." Enzo says.

"And you four are what? Going to stay here and teach for the next four years?"

"If that's what it takes." Kai states, and I look at Jett waiting for him to comment. Instead, he is hiding in the shadows.

"What about your territories? Your people? your families? You can't put all that on hold for me." I almost say, I am not worth it, but manage to keep it to myself.

"Our families are fine, and we created a sort of council of all four territories to help keep them running smoothly. No one knows the true reason we are here." Kai states.

"And why do they think you are here?" I dare ask.

"To train our own soldiers to fight against the shadow rebels." Enzo answers. I palm my face, trying to push back the headache forming from all the information.

"Why would you go through all this?" I feel warm hands on my shoulders and find two pools of blue looking at me.

"Because you belong to us. And we protect what's ours." Kai says before pulling me into a kiss. I open myself to him, clasping my hands behind his neck and pulling him closer to me. He breaks the kiss and presses his forehead to mine. "You will have to choose one of us, eventually but until that day, we will share you. If that is what you wish."

Reluctantly I let him step away from me. All four of them standing in different poses, watching, waiting, seeking an answer to a question I do not think I have one for.

"And all of you agreed to this?" I look between my two blood elves.

"I don't want any part in this. If we were to marry, it would be purely diplomatic." Xander growls and his words cut me. I remember the way he kissed me, and confusion is all I feel. He is hot and cold towards me.

"Don't be a dick, Xander. Besides, we all saw the way you kissed her so don't stand there and act like you don't feel something towards her." Jett growls. He prowls towards me, pulling me to my feet before claiming me with an aggressive kiss. Sucking on my bottom lip before biting it. Not hard enough to draw blood, but enough to cause a slight surge of pain.

"You're mine Red, I won't let you get away from me. I hope you know that." There was a pleading notion in his dark blues.

"Okay." Is all I can muster when it comes to him.

"Now, you will meet here to practice all your elements and druid magic. Seeing as druids are closest to mages, Xander will collaborate with you on that as well as your earth magic." Jett says, letting me go, just enough so our shoulders can brush up against each other.

"I will help you with your water magic." Kai says. "As well as teach you some of the benefits of being a rogue. For starters, throwing daggers from one-hundred yards away. And moving like a wraith." It's hard to believe that a rogue can be deadly and gentle at the same time. Kai has a way of easing my fears, rather than triggering any nightmares I have previously had about rogues.

QUEEN OF KINGS

"So, what you are saying is, on top of all my other training, I have to come train some more? When will I sleep?" I ask.

"We can set a schedule. But if you do not use your other elements, you may become complacent in them." Kai says, ever the sensible one.

"Alright, fine. But as soon as I am ready, even before the four years is up, I am taking my throne back. As for the marriage part, I'm not sure I am comfortable with that. I will have to think about it." I do not tell them that the truth is, my soul seems to be calling to all of them, including Xander and his mood swings. I do not think I will be able to choose, which means, I will not marry any of them. Besides, a queen can rule without a king. I would be the first, but if it comes down to it, I must choose myself.

"Are we agreed?" Kai asks. I look at all of them before speaking.

"Yes. But I do have conditions."

"Tell us." Enzo encourages.

"You will treat me like a regular student outside these four walls. I have already been accused of getting on my knees for a professor and I do not need the extra attention. Second, when I am here, we train. Got it?" They all nod. "Good. By the way Enzo, are you dating a student?"

"What?" By the look of surprise on his face, I can picture him spitting out a drink at my question.

"Are you sleeping with a student?" I ask.

"No, Ria, I swear." He speaks.

"Seems like someone has a little crush on you. Watch out for Melody the mouthy blood elf. She has eyes for you." Before I know what is happening, Enzo has me by my hips, pushing me against the wall, snarling at me.

"You think I have eyes for someone other than you?" he growls. "Let me remind you of who I want." I do not get a chance to protest before he crashes his lips to mine, adding fire to the heat. Smoke feels my mouth with the taste of him as he pushes me harder into the wall. I can feel him hardening against my stomach.

He breaks our kiss, leaning into my ear to whisper. "Do you feel that?

That should be proof enough of who I want."

I am speechless by the sudden aggression coming from my fire rogue. Jett claps, making me flinch slightly as Enzo backs away from me.

"Everyone should head to their rooms. We will need rest." Xander grumbles.

"See you in two days, Red." Jett winks, leaving me momentarily confused. "Don't tell me you aren't trying out for your house team?"

"I hadn't thought about it."

"Now you are. It will help you blend in more." He winks. One by one we exit the secret room and I clutch my book to my chest as I walk out of the library down the path that connects to Training North and then turn to Hunter House.

I finally make it back to my room, locking the door before falling onto my bed. Clutching my necklace, I close my eyes and send an update to Master Runk.

"You'd probably be pissed at me. I know you wouldn't approve of the four kings and their claim on me. Or at least three of them. Xander seems to be unsure of what he wants, and I for one don't need that right now." I sigh and continue my one-sided conversation. "I miss you Master. I know that if you were here, you would be able to guide me better. Perhaps I wouldn't be in this situation."

Fatigue starts to settle over me, and my eyes stay closed. The weight of the past few days sending me calmly into the dark abyss.

.

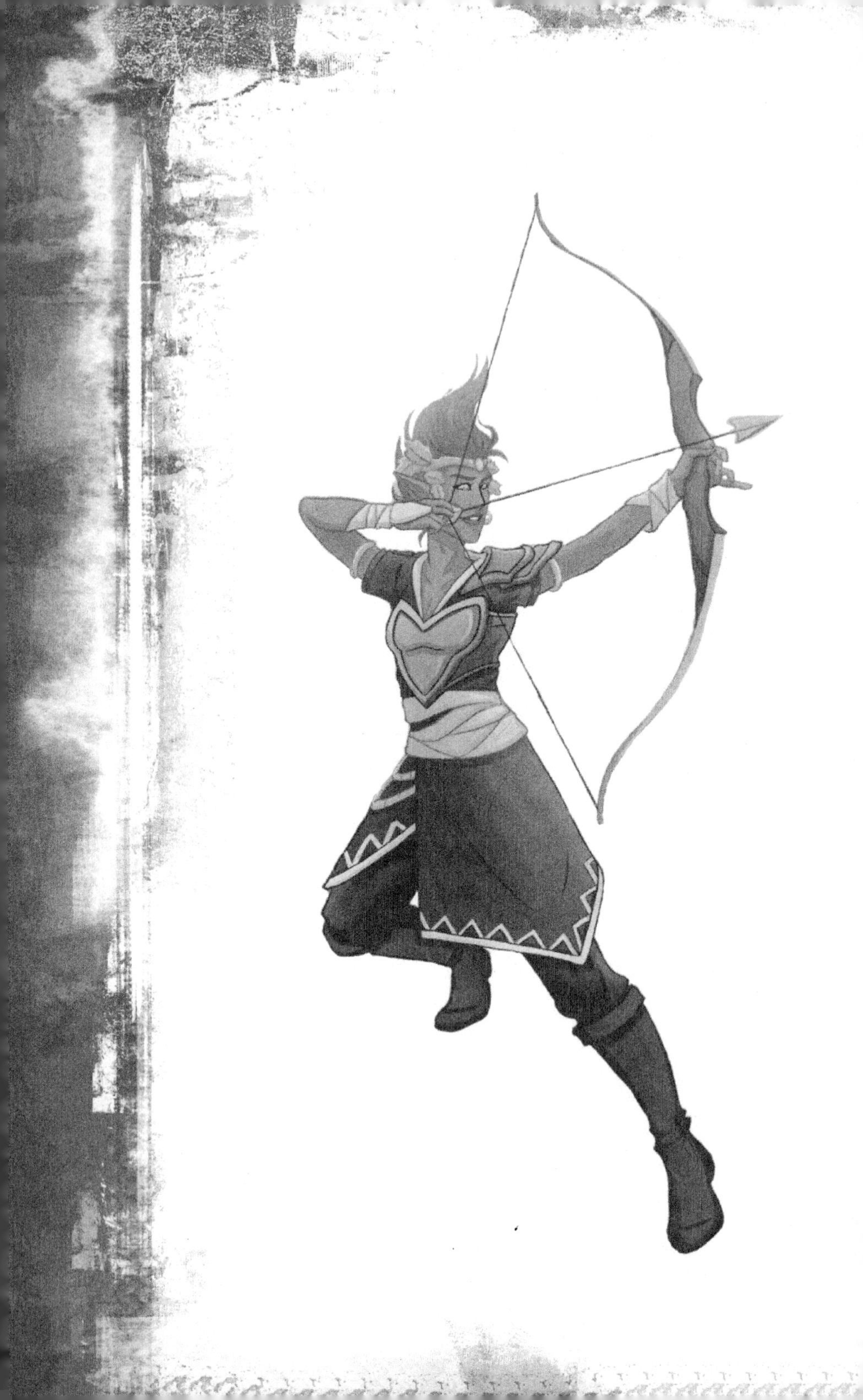

Chapter Thirteen

RIALYNNE

The next two days go by without any incidents, and I try to familiarize myself with the school map, ensuring I have charted out my routes to and from each class according to my schedule. It's pretty easy since all my classes are in Training South. My fire element and hunter classes are held in this hall, and combat class, which is what I am looking forward to the most, is at Training North.

Pulling on my uniform, I admire the detail that went into crafting it. The length is past my knees. The trim of the dress is decorated in golden triangles, and the ivory sash and leggings complement its crimson color. I pull on the ivory hand guards, each with a red diamond sewn on the top, and I adorn my crimson leather boots, completing the look.

Looking in the full-length mirror attached to the back of my door, I place my necklace underneath my top. Not to hide it, but just to keep it safe. We do have tryouts today and I do not want to remove it. Plus, there is no safer place than around my neck. Running my fingers over my tiara, I sigh, and a phantom pain from the day I lost my hearing pulses in my head.

What if it gets knocked off? Then everyone will know. Shaking off the worry, I open my door and head down to the lobby. A few students are socializing, and I walk past, wanting to avoid unwanted attention. The bright side of having my own room is that I can hide away and avoid any awkward conversations.

I have managed to avoid Mouthy Melody so far, although I have heard her boasting about her (not-so) secret relationship with the fire king. I can't help but roll my eyes at the audacity of her.

"Look who came out of her little cave." *Shit*, just when I thought I could avoid this bitch forever. Turning around, I see her, adorned in her fire uniform, her black hair tied back in a high up-do. "Has the hermit whore finally come out to play?" Her lackies seem to find her hilarious.

She flips her hair over her shoulder before checking out her nails.

Ares is she serious?

"I am a rare sight to see, but don't let my beauty scare you. It's natural for you to feel envious when you have to look at your own reflection every day."

"You got one thing right, Melody. You are a rare sight to see. But not because of your looks, but because I have never seen a blood elf with a mouth quite as big as yours." It may be immature of me to verbally fight with her, but if she knew who I was, I imagine she would treat me differently. That is the thing about both elves, and humans-some are straightforward, but others like to hide behind a mask, acting as if they are better than everyone around them.

"Your insults are as weak as your personality." She bites back.

"Right, I don't have time for this." Turning on my heel, I begin to make my way out the door when I feel my head ripped backwards. "I didn't say you could leave," She growls.

"This is your only warning, get your hands off me." I calmly say. She laughs in my ear.

"You think I am scared of you, first-year?" That was all I needed to hear before I thrust my elbow back, causing her to double over bringing her face straight into my knee. When she is on the floor, I look at the gathered crowd of hunters and shrug my shoulders.

"And that, my friends, is a lesson on what not to do." Antoinette's voice comes from behind them. The crowd parts for her as she walks up to see my handy work. "You better learn your place, Melody."

She grabs my hand, and we head straight out the door. We walk, arms locked, in silence, as we make our way to the Chow Hall. I look over at her and see her dressed in the same uniform as I am, except hers is blue, for her water elements, and she is sporting a golden headband as well. It's different from mine, but I still have the urge to ask her why she was not wearing it when I met her the first day.

"Toni," she stops abruptly, and I get the feeling I should not have called her that. "I'm sorry." She wraps her muscled arms around me squeezing me hard.

"Don't be, we are friends. You can call me by any nickname you choose." She pulls back and has the brightest smile.

"Okay, I need to ask you a question." We start walking again and she signals for me to continue. "Why are you wearing that?"

"It's a part of my uniform. Much like I assume yours is, only mine is for my status as a Lady of the Court of the Oceaniansphere."

"What? Are you related to King Kai?" I could not help asking her because the only way you can be a lady or lord is if you have any relation to the king or queen of that said court.

"Yeah, he is my cousin on my Mother's side." She answers as if it is not a big deal, but it is to me. Especially since I was engaged to him, and I have kissed him a few times.

"Wow, does that mean I have to bend the knee and 'say yes milady?'" We both laugh because I cannot imagine she fancies that idea. "Does everyone know?"

"Yes, but they also know that it doesn't grant me any special treatment. That's the way I like it." My respect for this female has grown ten-fold. A noble that does not care about her title. It is how I think it should be. Respect should be earned because of how you treat others, not because of your status.

The aroma of cooked meats and fruit makes my stomach growl as we enter through the Chow Hall doors. Long tables are spread throughout and are already filled with students. Everyone has the same uniform as me, except in their own elemental colors. The males have a different style, with pants instead of leggings.

"Hey, Toni, Ria." Damarias waves at us at the beginning of the food line.

"Good morning, Damarius." I say with a smile, and I see a blush rise in his cheeks.

"Move along, Dam. We are hungry." I look at Toni and smile. "What? He calls me Toni and I call him Dam."

"You two seem like great friends." We move down, the server slapping some eggs on my tray before I move down to the ham and roasted potatoes.

"Like I said the other day, we grew up together. We are friends." She says with a wink. After piling my tray high with various fruits, I grab a cup of coffee and follow Damarius to a vacant table at the front right of the hall, just off the side of the entry doors.

"Are you trying out for Hunter House?" Damarias ask before taking a bite of potato.

"That is the plan." I speak.

"We are going to kill it." Toni exclaims. I smile before biting into a juicy strawberry. I practically moan at the sweet flavor of it.

"Have you never had a strawberry before?" Toni asks.

"No, I grew up on meats and cheeses. Not much fruit around the…" I pause, not wanting to reveal that I grew up in the Cathedral. That would warrant too many questions.

"Where did you grow up?" Damarias asks.

"Here." I say not really lying. Klestria is my home.

"Like in the city?" Toni asks.

"Yeah." Still not a lie, considering the Cathedral is within the city of Klestria. A tingling sensation rushes over me and the entire hall goes deadly silent. I do not have to turn around to know why. My kings. Each of their scents hit me, and I cannot help but turn to look at them.

"If I wasn't into females, I might give myself to them for a night." Damarias states, almost making me spit my water out. "Me too." Toni says, it seems like they have that effect on the entire student body. Jett's eyes land on me, giving me a knowing smirk. They are all dressed in their designated elements, each wearing sleeveless shirts that leave their muscles clearly on display.

"King Enzo," Mouthy fucking Melody is jumping up and down waving at him. I growl. "Over here."

"Ria, you okay?" Toni asks, giving me a concerned look. No, I want to tell that bitch who Enzo belongs to, but I cannot. He shoots me an apologetic look before joining the other three in the line.

"She is such a needy bitch." I say before taking an aggressive bite from my bread. If I do not have something in my mouth, I will tell the bitch off.

"That's Melody for you." Damarias states.

"You act like you know her that well." They exchange glances, and a revelation hits me. "No way. She grew up with you too?"

"Yep. Three years our senior but she was just like that in the village." Toni states.

"But you are a lady of the court." I state. "True, but like I said, she was like that growing up. Trying to befriend anyone and everyone that was connected to the court."

"She tried to be your friend?" I ask.

"Yep. At first, I gave her the benefit of the doubt, she showed her true intentions. I caught her peeking in on Kai when he was undressing. Had the guards throw her out and threaten her with imprisonment if she ever dared to step foot in the court again." I bursts out laughing, earning a few looks, but I don't care because, really that's fucking hilarious.

"You should've thrown her in prison. Might have been good for her." I laugh again. We continued our small talk, making me forget about the four kings for a while. After breakfast, I made my way to our secret spot in the library. Once inside, I notice I am alone, so I pull my book out of my bag and begin reading it.

"What language is this?" I ask out loud. The entire book is written in it, and it infuriates me. Slamming the book closed, I toss it on the cushion next to me before getting up, and scrubbing my hands down my face. Two arms wrap around my waist, and I smell Jett's airy scent.

"Do you need to relax?" he growls in my ear before nipping it.

"Maybe," I tease before looking up at him over my shoulder. Reaching up to run my fingers through his silky hair, and pull him down to kiss me. It starts out soft, but it quickly intensifies until he has me pinned to the wall, his hands palming my breasts. His hand wanders to the waistband of my legging before dipping further down, finding me already dripping.

"Always ready," he growls.

"Jett," he kissed me as he circled my clit.

"What do you want, Red?"

"You."

"I'm going to need you to elaborate."

"I need you. Inside me. Now." I growl before tugging at his waist band.

"What's going on?" Kai's voice does not make Jett stop, instead he smiles at me before turning to look at Kai.

"Relaxing, Red. She needs release. Want to join?" I gasp as he slips a finger inside me. "Would you like that, Red? You want us both, don't you?"

"Yes." I moan. Then look at Kai as he swallows hard. "Kai, please."

"Don't deny our queen. Come and taste how sweet she is." Jett says as he takes his hand out my pants leaving me panting. I watch as Kai walks over, taking Jett's coated fingers and then seductively licking them before letting out a growl.

I run my eyes down his body and stop at the bulge in his pants. "You want me, Ria?"

"Yes." I say, as I reach for him. Jett steps aside and lets Kai come in for a deep kiss. They start pulling my clothes off me until I am bare before them. Jett kneels before me and begins to devour my pussy as Kai pulls my nipple into his mouth. I scratch at Kai's tunic, urging him to take it off.

He releases my breast to remove it and I run my hands down his chiseled abdominal muscles before slipping it past his waistband and gripping his cock. Jett continues his assault on my pussy, and I am so close.

"Please," I beg and Kai quiets me with a kiss as I pump him up and down. "Jett."

"Cum for me." he growls then bites my clit, drawing blood. My orgasm rushes through me, and I moan into Kai's mouth.

Jett stands up, his mouth coated in my release and blood. "Do you want to taste her?"

He asks Kai who looks hungry for it. I expected him to lick my sensitive pussy, but he ran his tongue across Jett's mouth, making my need for them both intensify.

"You taste so fucking good, Ria." Kai growls before kissing me and then picking me up. I wrap my legs around his waist as he moves us to the couch. He sets me down before standing next to Jett. They strip down and get on either side of me. Jett's behind me while Kai kisses me. "Do you want to taste my blood again?" Jett asks as he trails kisses down my neck.

"Yes." I managed to say.

"How about with Kai's cock in your pussy? Would you like that?" He asks. I just nod. Kai sits down on the couch, running his hand up and down his shaft. "Sit!"

I move and straddle Kai. He runs his tip along my wet folds before I sink down on him.

"Fuck, you're so tight." Kai groans.

"Look at me, Red," Jett says, and I look at him before he kisses me, hard. It's never soft with Jett. "I'm going to give you a taste of my blood, but then I'm fucking you here." He runs his fingers over my tight hole. "Can you manage two cocks at once?"

"Yes."

"Good girl. Kai, some water magic would help. Our Queen needs some lubrication if I am going to fit." He says before giving me his wrists and I feel the cool flow of water swirling around my ass. It's a new sensation and then I feel Jett insert two fingers, stretching me while Kai's magic aids him. After he inserts a third, I damn near cum again.

Kai begins to fuck me with hard thrusts while I pierce my fangs into Jett's wrists, pulling his blood down my throat, sending me into overdrive. While I drink from Jett, his hand moves to my clit. He begins circling it as Kai continues to fuck me.

I release Jett's wrist before kissing him. He breaks our kiss, pushing me forward so I can kiss Kai.

"Cum for me, Ria." Kai demands. With one more circle of his finger, my release follows, and I clench down around him. He pauses, but Jett adds another finger, fucking my ass through my climax.

"Good girl. You can take it." Jett praises before pulling his fingers out. I catch my breath and I wonder why Kai has not started moving again. Suddenly I feel Jett's tip pressing at my other entrance. "Relax, Red."

I do as he says, and he pushes in, causing me to clench around Kai who groans. Once Jett is fully seated inside me, I sit back, and he reaches around to flick my nipple.

They begin to move, in a perfect rhythm. Picking up speed, their bodies pressed to me, lips all over me, with fingers on my sensitive clit, it is too much as I feel another orgasm about to explode from me.

"You are going to cum for us." Jett says as he nips my ear. He pinches my clit and I scream as I clench around both of their cocks, milking them as they both grunt and cum inside me.

As we all come down from our high, Jett lifts me off Kai before easing out of me. They clean me up then themselves and before sandwiching me on the floor.

"That was amazing." I say as my eyelids droop close.

"Indeed, it was." Kai says before kissing me.

"Now we just need the other two." Jett smugly says, I wonder if I could manage it. "Are you relaxed, Red?"

"Very. But if I don't perform well at tryouts, it's your fault." I say pointing at them both.

"You will do fine. If not, I know the coach and you just made the team." Jett says before kissing my neck.

"What did I say about special treatment?" I scolded him.

"I'd say fucking your professors is special treatment. What about you Kai?"

"Yes. Besides, you are our queen. You deserve everything we have to give." My heart flutters at his honesty.

"Get some sleep, Red. Tryouts are in a couple hours." Jett says and my eyes flutter closed as sleep finds me.

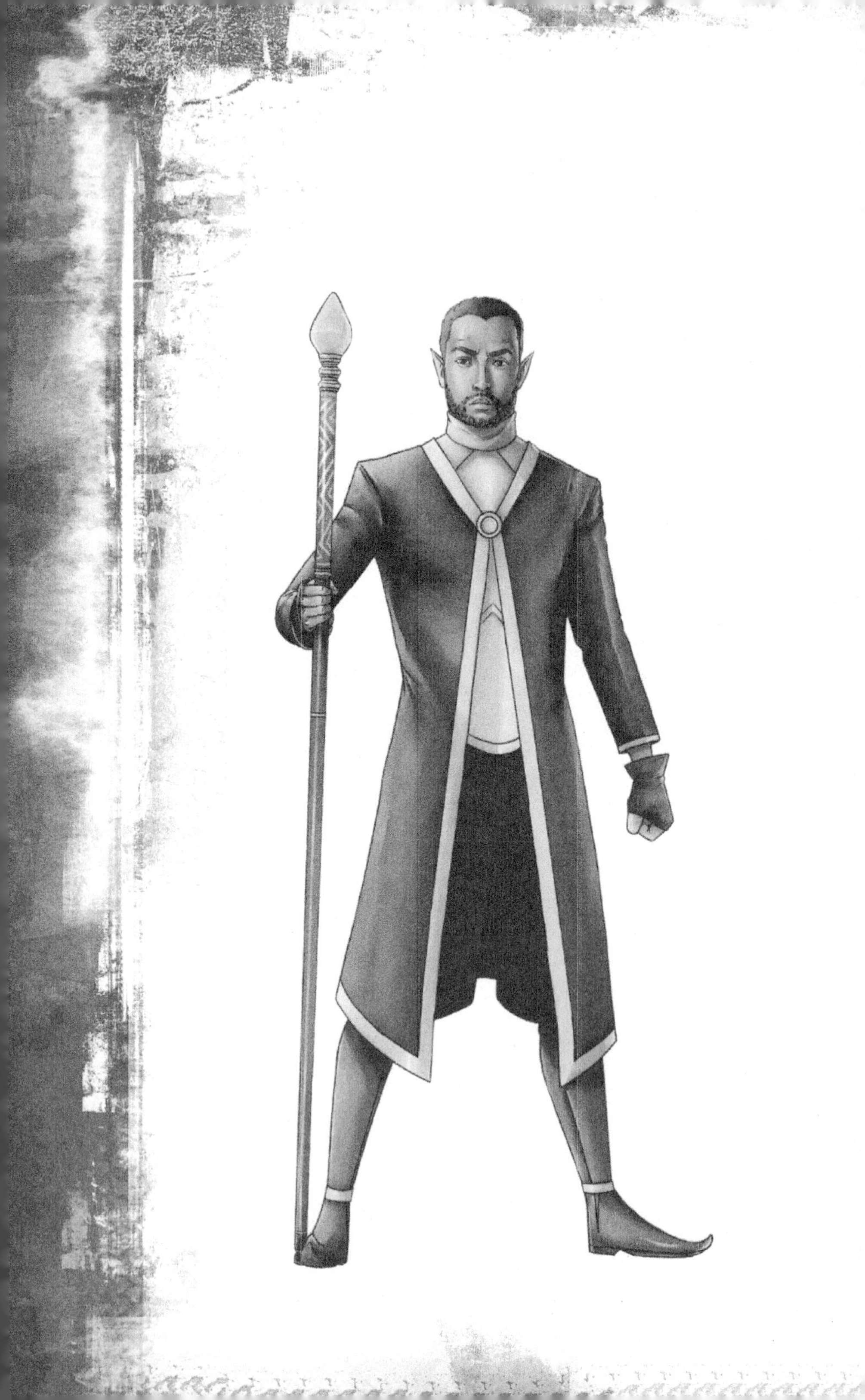

Chapter Fourteen

XANDER

The magical alarm vibrated in my pants notifying me that someone had entered our secret spot in the library. I pulled out my device and watched the feed. I have not told the others about me placing a camera in there, and I do not think what I saw would have happened if I had.

Rialynne was reading that same book again before Jett showed up. I watched as he pinned her to the wall and began finger fucking her. I was glad to be in my room as I watched as Kai and Jett double team her, and wow, she fucking enjoyed it. Her moans and naked body had me pulling out my cock. As Jett fucked her ass, I imagined me there instead, feeling her tight hole milking my cock.

I stroked myself harder as I watched, grunting her name as I exploded in my hand at the same time as the other two did.

What the fuck is wrong with me?

After cleaning myself up, I saw them asleep, cuddled on the floor together. Putting my device away, I decided to get Enzo, so we can head to our spot.

"What's up man?" He seems to have just woken up as his shaggy brown hair is disheveled and his chest is bare.

"We need to head to the spot, and set boundaries with Rialynne." I told him. He sighs before signaling for me to come in. I close the door and wait as he dresses.

"Look man, I have a lot of respect for you, but I'm pretty sure it's too late for that."

"No, there is still time. Unless you fucked her too?" I am not sure I want to know the answer.

"No, but that doesn't mean I don't want to." He answers, brushing his hair.

"That's what I mean. We can't start having a relationship with her. She is under our protection."

"I get that, but you can't sit there and tell me that if she wanted your cock, you would deny her." No, I would not, but he does not need to know that, so I stay silent. "I saw the way you kissed her man. None of us are fooled."

"That was a moment of weakness. I just haven't been laid in a while." I tell him.

"Whatever man, we can talk with the others, but if Ria wants to fuck me, I'm not stopping her."

"Then what's the point?"

"I don't know." He shrugs.

"Let's just go." I storm out, not bothering to look back to see if he is following me. This female will ruin us. Chew all of us up and spit us on the ground. It might be too late for Jett and Kai, but I can still save Enzo and myself. I just need to have a word alone with her.

When we walk through the invisible barrier, I see they are all three still naked asleep. Using my earth magic, I send a tremor under them, jolting them awake.

"What the fuck, Xander?" Jett growls.

"That's what I want to know. Have you two gone fucking mad?" I do not even spare Rialynne a glance. I know what will happen if I see her naked body. Just thinking about it has my dick hardening again. "Get the fuck up and get dressed. We need to talk."

Enzo steps through and freezes, his eyes trailing over the three of them. "Damn, seems like I missed all the fun."

"Guess you will have to join the next time." Jett winks as they all get dressed.

"What's up?" Kai asks.

"You tell me." I say pointing at the female in question.

"Are you jealous?" Jett taunts.

"Why would I be jealous?" I say, adding insult to the injury.

"Because we got a taste of her sweet cunt, and you didn't." Jett seems pissed, but I am one second from putting him in his place.

"Don't you see what she is doing? She is spreading her fucking legs for you. Reeling you in. When it's time for her to take back the throne, you will be left in the mud. She's just another whore." I hear Rialynne gasp, before Jett attacks.

Adding air magic to each of his punches, to increase the power of them, he punches me until I can taste the copper tang of my blood in my mouth. I bring my knee up to his gut with a shin-guard of earth to add to it. I get to my feet as his back hits the wall. He charges for me, but we both freeze.

A wall of green flames coming from Rialynne, halting both Jett and me, splitting the room.

"Knock it off, or you will take this entire place down with your temper tantrums." She growls at us. Her flames are not hurting us, and I am going to assume it is the druid magic that is aiding in that. "Xander if you are so pissed off that I have a sexual relationship with them, then you will have to get over it, because I am my own person and I can fuck who I want when I want."

"You'll destroy us all and Zavinia." I growl before walking off.

"Dude, calm down." Enzo says as he steps in front of me.

"Back down."

"Not until you tell me what is actually going on."

I glance back watching as Rialynne tends to Jett's wounds, a surge of jealousy making me angry at the fact that she is not doing that for me.

"I said back off!" I push him aside and then walk out, not caring about the protest that follows, just needing to get out of there before more shit happens. There is only one person I can go to that will help me figure out what the fuck is wrong with me.

I step out of the portal into my father's house that connects to the castle grounds. It's quiet which is to be expected at this time of day. The scent of disease and death linger in the air, making my stomach churn.

"Xander?" I hear his weak voice calling out from his room.

"Hey Pops," I say as I walk over to him. My heart squeezes at the sight of him lying in his bed. The once healthy dark pigment of his skin is now gone as the disease attacks his body.

"Come here, boy. It's been too long." He is right about that. I have not seen him since Rialynne first left to go to the academy.

"Are you taking your medicine?" I ask as I place a kiss on his forehead.

"Yes." He wheezes, followed by a coughing fit. I clench my fists, hating seeing him like this. My father was the most powerful king and earth mage in all of Zavinia before he fell to this illness. Blood Poison is an incurable disease that attacks all the body's organs. When he first fell ill, we thought it would pass because it's exceedingly rare for an elf to get sick.

Unlike humans, our immunity is superior.

Everything seemed fine until he was found, passed out on the floor, with blood dribbling from his mouth.

The Healers diagnosed him with blood poison, meaning someone tampered with the royal blood supply. We still have not figured out who. I questioned all the servants, but none were found guilty.

"You look upset, tell Pops what's wrong? Is it the female you spoke of?" I smile at him before nodding. "Don't keep a dying man waiting. I need to know if my son will have his queen soon."

"Not likely, Pops."

"Hogwash, she'd be a fool not to marry you, Xander. You are the best person I have ever known. So honorable and devoted to your duties." His praise makes tears swell in my eyes. I do not know what I will do when he leaves me, how I will rule without his support and guidance.

"Thanks Pops, but she hates me." I told him. I would never lie to my father. I see no reason for it.

"Why? Did you do something?" I laugh but he narrows his silver-gray eyes.

"Yeah, I've kind of been an asshole to her."

"Then fix it. There is still time, I'm sure of it."

"I don't know Pops, seems to me like she likes the others more." I tell him with a shrug.

"I see. Have you tried telling her the truth?"

"No, because every time I am around her, we just argue."

"Son, do you think my marriage with your mother didn't go without its fair share of arguments?" A tear falls from his eyes at the memory of her.

Mom passed giving birth to my baby brother. "Mom adored you."

"That she did, but you know why?" I shook my head. "Because I put forth the effort to make her happy. Every second of every day, even when we fought, I did what I could to make it right between us. That is what you do for the person you love. The one that completes you. When you have found your mate." I let his words sink in before kissing his forehead again.

"Thanks Pops, you should rest."

"You bring her here to see me once you have made it right between the two of you."

"Yes, Sir." I walk out, glancing back at him as he falls asleep. I slink down on the sofa in his living room, staring at the ceiling as the weight of the world slams into me. *What am I going to do without you, Pops?*

A knock sounds, snapping me awake and I realize I must have dozed off. Getting up, I make my way to the door.

"Good evening, Majesty." Lady Rose curtseys before pushing through the door with her medicine bag. She is a short human with brown hair and fair skin, wearing her healer uniform covering her from neck to feet.

"Good evening, how is Pops doing?" I asked as I shut the door.

"Not good, if you want an honest answer." She states, setting her bag down and opening it.

"How long?" I need to know. I have to prepare myself and Xavier." My little brother works in Vain Prison as the warden. I haven't seen him since Father became ill. Our relationship is estranged to say the least.

"Months, maybe less." She sighs, and I can see the grief on her face. Rose is one of Zivania's most powerful healers. She has been tending to Pops since he fell ill one year ago. "Thanks, keep me updated." I told her.

"I will. Have you found the culprit?" She asks as she pulls vials of medicine out before entering Pop's room. She stops in the door frame, watching him sleep.

"No, but I suspect it could have been a shadow rebel. A rogue. They are the only ones with the skill to slip in and out of places unnoticed. What I do not understand is why? Why did they attack him? Pops is the best king in all of Zavinia." There is pain and anger in my tone, but Rose knows it is not directed towards her.

"I don't know, but we will figure it out. I am getting close to finding out the source of the poison." I know Rose has been collaborating with other healers to determine what the main ingredients used, but it has not been easy. Most poison comes from basic plants, but none are powerful enough to take down a powerful elf mage. At least none in the Magianinasphere.

"Thank you. I have to go, but I will be back soon." She nods before entering Pop's room. I look back once more before summoning a portal back to Klestria Academy. I step directly into our secret room, seeing it vacant and back in order.

"I'm sorry." I fell to my knees and let all my emotions from seeing my father hit me.

"I'm sorry."

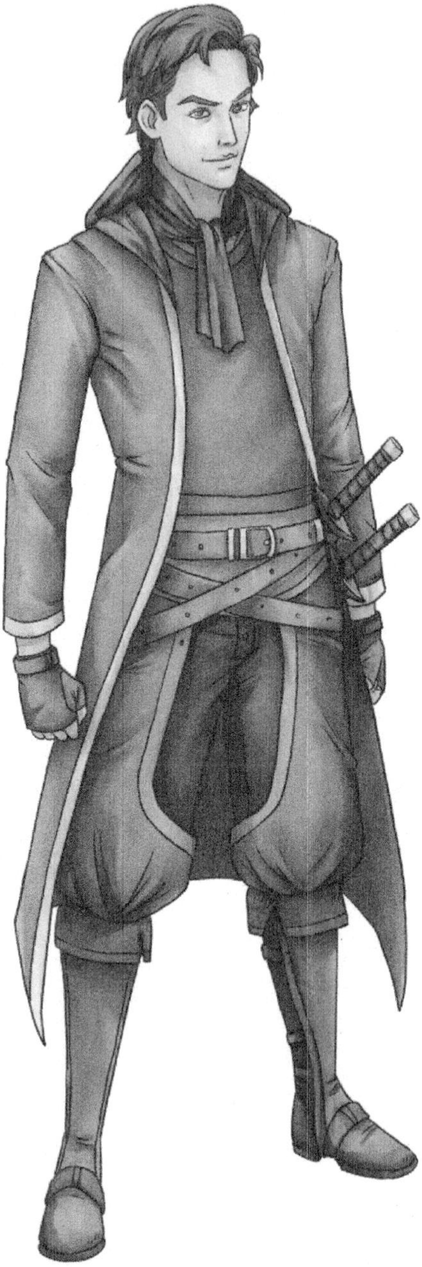

Chapter Fifteen

ENZO

I watch the bleachers circling the stadium as all the students huddle in their designated house section. Irfu is a sport that I enjoyed playing when I came here as a student. Time works differently here in the academy; at least ten years ago in the outside world. The other kings were here at the same time.

Ria is technically too old to attend, but since she is a blood elf, twenty-eight may as well be eighteen in the eyes of us humans. Thinking of her, I spot her standing next to a tall brunette from the Hunter House. I assume she is her friend because I see them hanging around a lot.

"Listen up assholes, these are tryouts. If you want to make your house team, then you better bring your game. Irfu is not a dainty sport, only the toughest of the tough can make it. Use of powers is encouraged." I can see Jett is enjoying his position as coach. "Ten versus ten. Hunter and Mage will go first. The ball will be thrown between the two pitchers, then the games begin."

He blows a whistle and I see an intimidated expression come across Ria's face. Getting to my feet, I cannot resist teasing her. Her back is to me as she gets in a fighting position.

"You have no clue what you are doing, do you?" She flinches, and I smile at her.

"What are you doing here?"

"Eyes forward. I'm here to make sure you don't get pummeled too badly." I tell her. "The ball can't go forward; it has to go diagonal or backwards. There are five offensive players and five defensive players. The defenders are the back five and offenders are the front five. If you get knocked out of bounds, you are eliminated until the next round. The goal is to put the ball in the net. Each goal is worth five points, and the first team to score two-hundred points wins."

"Am I an offender?" she asks.

"Yes, which means the pitcher can't throw it to you. It makes you a bigger target because the fewer offenders, the smaller the chance for the other team to score."

"And I need to protect the pitcher?" she asks.

"Precisely." I wink.

"Enzo, get off my fucking field." Jett yells.

"Good luck." I make my way back to the bleachers and watch as the games begin. Jett blows the whistle and throws the ball. Jumping in the air, the Hunter pitcher grabs it and moves forward, dodging the Mage pitcher. My eyes land on Ria who is in a fight with one of the water elementals. Steam spurts up from the opposing elements meeting.

"Move it." Jett yells. Ria manages to knock the human water elemental out of bounds before running to guard the pitcher. Damn, seeing her aggressive side is turning me on and it is not exactly appropriate for me to have a hard-on.

"How's our queen doing?" Kai asks from beside me.

"Shit, when did you get here?" I ask him. He smiles.

"Like five seconds before you started adjusting your cock." He smirks. "It's okay, I know it's hard not to get turned on when she is around."

"Right. She just knocked that human out. She is really getting the hang of tackling these fuckers to the ground."

"I see that." I look and see Ria has just elbowed some blood elf girl in the chin. Blood flows from the girl's chin as she curses her.

"You are all weak pathetic losers." Jett yells and I cannot help but laugh. The man has a passion for the game, and that is honorable. "Move your ass, Red."

I see her getting up from the dirt, defending herself against another earth elemental. The pitcher has lost the ball to the other team. I realize that the only offender of the Hunter House left is Ria. It's five against one, not really fair, but our queen can manage it.

Ria looks at all five of them, breathing heavily, before charging forward. Bending just as the earth elemental shoots rocks at her head. She hits him in the chest with a fireball before sweeping his feet out. Not even glancing back at him, she moves on to her next target, taking a punch to the jaw, before knocking them on their ass.

Watching her fight is like watching a dancer perform. The fluid and accuracy of her movements are unmatched. I know she is holding back, because if anyone found out she was an elite druid, her life would be in danger.

"Get that whore." the familiar high-pitched tone of Melody rings out from the student section.

"Isn't she in the Hunter House?" Kai whispers to me.

"Yes." I speak.

"Then why is she wanting them to take out Ria?" I shrug.

"Put that red-headed bitch in the dirt." She yells, and Jett's head snaps to her.

"Fuck, he's going to kill a student and get us all in trouble." I garble before getting to my feet.

"You got this?" Kai asks.

"Yep. The girl has a crush on me, remember?" He nods. I make my way over to her. "Melody, a word?"

"Oh, of course Your Majesty." She begins to move but I hold my hand up. "Nope, stand right where you are. I have a question." I pause and all eyes are on us. "Are you the head of the Hunter House?"

"Yes, Sire." She says, fluttering her lashes.

"Okay, then why the fuck are you cheering for the Mages?" She scoffs, so I continue. "Miss Faith is a fellow Hunter, which means you should be loyal to her, as she is playing for your house. Do you know what pisses a king off more than anything?"

She doesn't answer, too stunned to speak. "Disloyalty. Would you like to be thrown in prison?" She shakes her head, tears running down her cheeks. "Good, now cheer for your team or get the fuck out of this stadium."

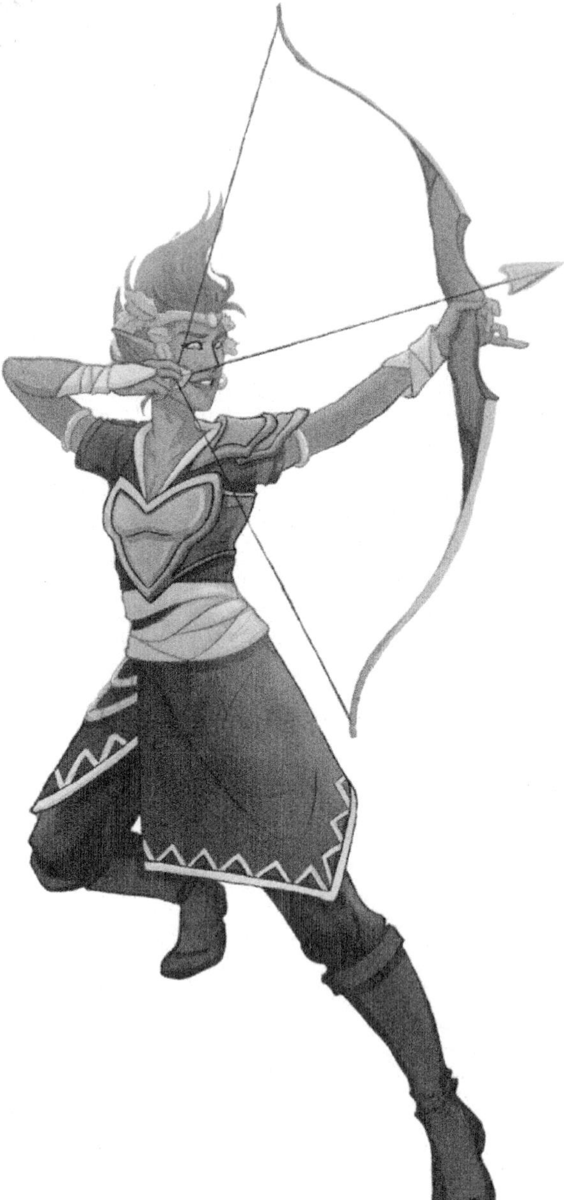

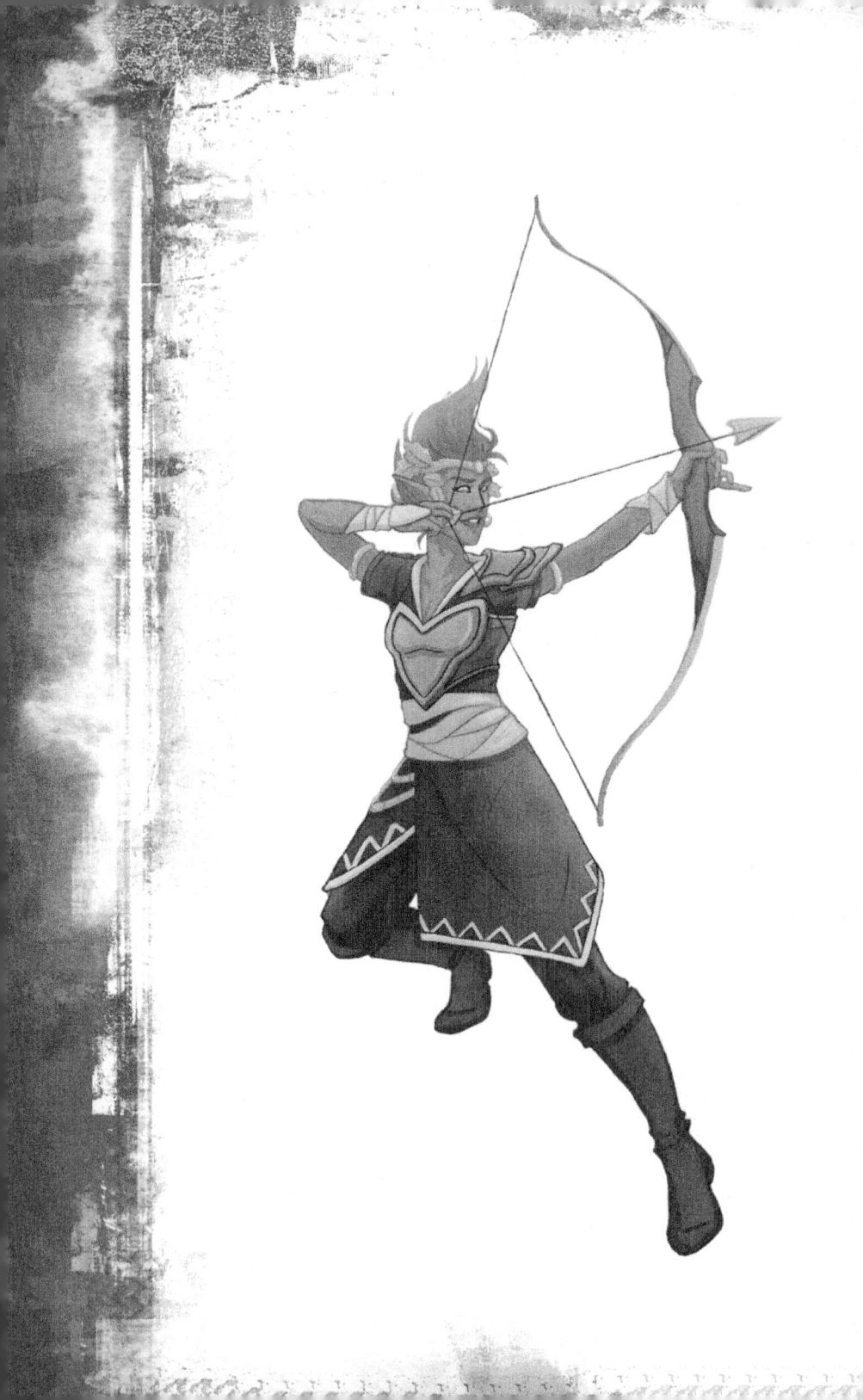

Chapter Sixteen

RIALYNNE

I watch as Enzo chews Melody's ass out for being the bitch she is. The entire game seems to have paused as he does. A whistle blows, snapping us all out of our stupor.

"Finish it!" Jett yells.

I look at the pitcher and charge forward. We have almost made it to the five defenders standing in front of the goal, which means time to knock these assholes out is up. I use my fire magic to engulf my entire body, before tackling the pitcher. Which happens to be Damarias. He squeaks as I bring him down, yank the ball from his hand, and run towards the goal.

My teammates cheer me on as I run diagonally across the field. I eye the five mage defenders and plot my oath to the goal. Each are of a different element and moves to attack me at once. With the force of all the elements coming at me, I clear my mind. Allowing the flow of my druid magic to solidify my fire shield, and move through the field.

Flipping over the two middle defenders, I throw the ball straight into the net. The entire arena is silent as the goal alarm rings, and all the magic dissipates. I can't hear a thing. Suddenly I notice the missing weight on my head. My headband must have been knocked off at some point during their attack. Looking around, I start to freak out.

My breathing picks up and I feel a panic attack coming. My chest starts caving in. *They know. Fuck! How could I be so reckless?* Warm hands cup my face and I see two deep swirls of chocolate looking at me with concern. His earthy scent washes over me as I look into the eyes of the last person I would have expected to be here.

"Xander." I say. Or I think I say, as I cannot hear myself speak. His mouth is moving but I cannot make out the words. He makes an 'O' shape with his mouth, willing me to breathe. I feel myself calm down, and get to my feet. Looking around, I see everyone looking at me, Toni approaches me, handing me my broken headband.

She mouths what I think is a question, but I just turn and run. I do not know where I am going, just that I need to move. Suddenly, I am outside the gates of the academy, back at the front steps of the Cathedral. The moon is high in the sky as I look up at the tall building I grew up in. The need to see my ladies again makes me cry harder.

I put my broken band back on, trying to see if it will work. I do not know until I hear a distant voice. It comes in shaky, but I can make out the words.

"Are you okay, miss?" A soft voice comes from behind me.

"Yes, I just needed some air." I tell her not to look.

"Are you a student?" she asks, I look down and realize I am still in my filthy uniform. I forgot time moved faster outside the gates of the academy.

"Yes, Ma'am."

"Are you visiting your family?" I turn around, spotting who must be the source of the voice. An older human.

"No, I don't have a family." Hearing the words out loud breaks me.

"Would you like to have some tea and talk about it?" she asks.

"You seem overly sweet, but I really shouldn't go with a stranger. Plus, I should really be heading back to the academy. Classes start soon and I don't want to miss curfew."

"Okay. If you ever change your mind, my house is just over there." She points. I thank her again before starting my walk back to the academy. It takes a couple hours before I reach the iron gates again. My body is sore and weak, and I need blood and food.

When I walk through the gates, the only thing that changes is the position of the moon. It appears to have just risen, which means I missed the dinner hour. I start to walk past Training South when someone grabs me from behind.

"Get off me!" I try to scream but a hand is covering my mouth.

"Easy, Red." I hear as an airy scent hits me.

"Jett?" I ask.

"Stay quiet. I don't want anyone to see me dragging a student into the faculty hall." I know this is a terrible idea, but I do not have the energy to fight, and the smell of Jett's blood is calling to me.

He uses his air magic to quiet our steps as we make our way into the vacant Main Hall, down a few winding corridors into a circular room with four separate doors. He pulls me into what must be his and shuts the door. I freeze, seeing the other three sitting on a couch that is across from his bed.

"Your room is a lot bigger than mine." I say.

"The privilege of being a king. Now strip." He clearly does not want to talk about anything.

"Jett…"

"No. Shower first, then we'll talk. You missed dinner, and I know you need blood. Let me take care of you." We walk into his bathroom, and he strips out of his clothes before turning the water on. We get in, and he begins scrubbing me down. I rinse the body soap from myself, and shudder as he reaches for the shampoo. "I'm not going to hurt you, Red."

"Please, just don't." I beg him and then take my headband off. My world goes silent again as I reach for the shampoo, but Jett shakes his head, turning me around. I feel his fingers massaging my head, and I cannot help but moan at the way it feels. No one has ever touched my hair except my ladies, when they needed to fix it.

Once I am clean, he shuts the water off, and dries me off before grabbing one of his night shirts and pulls it over my head. He adorns some night pants, grabs my hand, and pulls me out to the area the other three kings are waiting. Kai gets up and rushes over, pulling me into a hug. He mouths something, but I cannot read his lips well.

Jett pulls me into a seat where a plate of food and a chalice of blood awaits me. He points at it and mouths the word 'eat.' I chew on the cooked chicken, and wash it down with the cold blood. I miss the warmth of taking it from the vein, but Jett seems to be pissed at me for running off. They do not understand, never will, and my headband is broken leaving me in silence again.

Jett pulls me from the seat, the second I finish and pushes me into the couch across the four of them. They all stand with their arms crossed over their broad chest waiting for an explanation that I cannot give them.

"I don't want to talk about it." I state. Confusion crosses their faces, but it is Xander who moves first, squatting so he is eye level with me, reminding me of the way he prevented my panic attack from coming. His calloused hand touches my cheek, and I close my eyes and lean into his warmth. This is the first time he has ever been gentle with me. I do not know how long my eyes are closed, but when I open them, they all seem to be trying to get my attention by saying my name or snapping their fingers near my ears.

I pull away from Xander, tears rolling down as I fall to the carpet on my knees, hiding the shame I feel for my disability on full display. My secret. My weakness. The constant reminder of the day I lost everything and everyone that I cared about.

Jett pulls my hands from my face and grips my chin, making me look at him. He is talking, but I cannot hear him, and I need to. I need to hear all their voices or I will feel alone even with them around me. Xander hands me something, and I gasp as I see it's my headband. I look at him and he nods. With shaky hands, I take it and place it on my head, using my magic to sink the prongs into the spot just above my ears.

"Ri...Ria...Rialynne," Xander's voice fills in my ears and I let out a whimper of relief.

"Thank you." I get to my feet and hug him. He wraps his arms around me, letting me hold him until I am ready to face them all. "I guess you have questions."

"Later, you need rest." Xander says and before pointing to Jett's bed. I crawl into the middle, Xander comes to my front. Jett climbs in behind me as the other two enter at my feet. "Sleep, Red, we will be here when you wake."

I feel warmth all around me as my eyes flutter open. Xander is still sleeping in front of me, but I feel Jett's morning erection digging in my ass. I turn onto my back and feel his lips brush my cheek.

"How are you feeling?" he whispers.

"Like I got beat up by ten people." I answered him.

"Here." He offers up his wrists and I greedily take it, savoring the warmth of his blood as it refuels my body and my magic.

"Better?"

"Yes, thank you."

"You should show me how grateful you are right now." He pushes his hardened cock towards my thigh, and I flush with heat.

"The others are still sleeping."

"I don't think they will mind waking up to watch you wrap your pretty little mouth around my cock. In fact, I think they would enjoy it." he smiles.

"No sex until she explains herself." Xander says with sleepy words. I sit up, and untangle myself from them, escaping to the bathroom to relieve myself. After washing my hands, I come out and find all four of them awake without their shirts on. Goddesses bless me.

"Why don't you start from the beginning?" Xander says, motioning for me to sit down.

"Fine, but you need clothes. I can't concentrate with all four of you half-naked."

"Are you dripping for us, Red?" Jett teases.

"Nope." I lied. He chuckles. As they dress and take their own bathroom trips, I sip on some water.

"As you know, my family was killed by a rogue assassin. That day, I was attacked too." I pause as the images from my six-year-old self-stare into the dark eyes of the killer. "They hit me on the back of my head hard enough to leave permanent damage. This," I reach up and run my hands over the now fixed metal. "Is a hearing aid. Without it, I am deaf."

My eyes drop at the confession. Two fingers tilt my chin up and I find myself staring into Kai's gentle eyes. I expect to see pity, but all I see is desire. "You don't get to feel ashamed; you understand me? You are a fucking Queen, Ria. Just because you are deaf does not make you any less sexy, powerful, or strong. You survived. You're a fucking warrior in my eyes."

"Kai's right, Red. You are the most powerful elemental to exist in a long time."

"Everyone should be on their knees worshiping you." Kai steps back and my heart rate increases as one by one, they kneel, all except Xander.

"You're my queen, Ria. I've told you that since the moment I saw you." Enzo says. But my eyes do not leave Xander's. He steps forward, looking down upon me, before he moves and kneels before me.

"You are the only person alive that I will ever *willingly* kneel to.

Rialynne Faith, you are my queen, and I will never allow you to berate or shame yourself for the trauma you survived." My breath catches as I watch these four powerful kings kneel before me. Devoting their loyalty to me. The deaf queen of Klestria. "I am nothing without my device." I say it too low for them to hear.

"We will train you to fight without it. I devote myself to you, Rialynne Faith. The true Queen of Zavinia." Xander exclaims. The three others follow suit.

"I don't know what to say." I am speechless. I do not know who moves first, but Xander pulls me to my feet as they surround me.

"Don't say anything, Red. Let us worship our Queen."

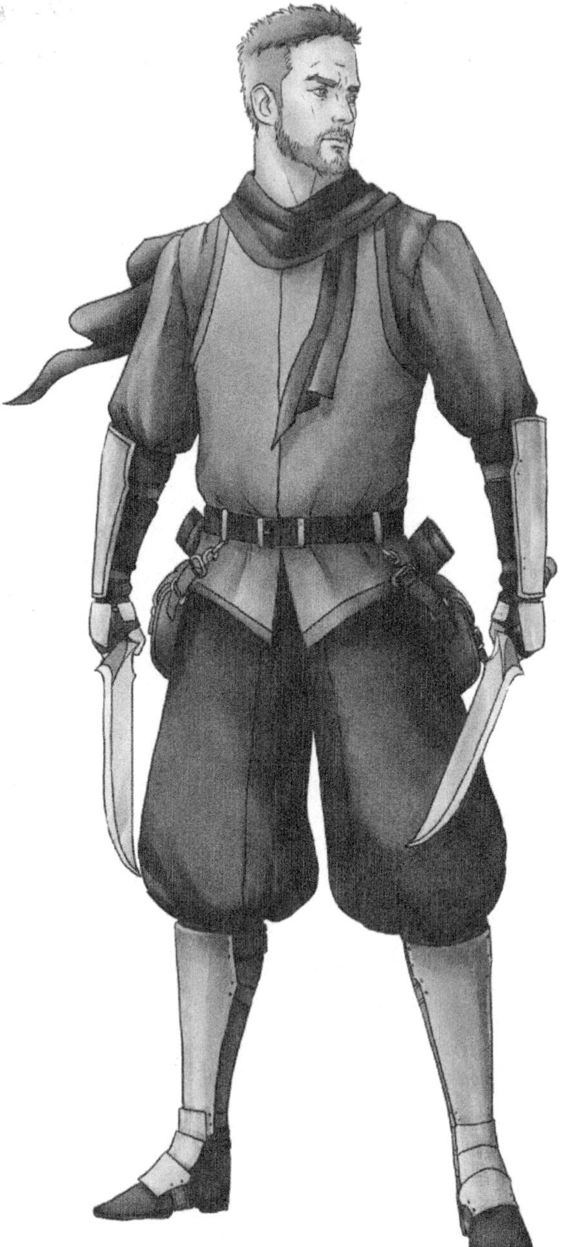

Chapter Seventeen

KAI

Xander moves first, crushing his lips to Ria as we start removing her clothes. They break apart so we can remove Jett's shirt from her body. Enzo kisses her next, while Xander moves his mouth to her left nipple, leaving room for me to take the right. Jett kneels in front of her pussy and begins to eat it.

"You're so beautiful, Ria." I tell her as I kiss her neck, palming her breast.

"Jett," she moans, and I watch as she grips his hair and shamelessly rides his face. While Jett brings her to her first climax, we step back and undress. I never thought I would share one woman with other men, but this is what makes her happy. I have always been attracted to both sexes.

I watch as she takes over pinching her nipples and I run my hand up and down my cock, soaking in the sight of her.

"Cum, Red." Jett growls and she practically screams but it is muffled as Xander kisses her again. Jett licks up her juices before stepping back to remove his clothes. I walk up to him, cup his face, and lick Ria's cum from his mouth before slipping my tongue between his soft lips.

"Are you going to fuck each other?" Ria says and steps back from Jett.

"If that's what you want. I'll take a cock." I told her.

"Tell us what you want, beautiful." Xander says as he lifts her into his arms.

"I want you and Enzo inside me while Kai takes Jett's cock in his mouth, and I take Kai's cock in mine." She says, I get even harder thinking about it. We pile onto Jett's bed, plotting how this will work.

"You need to cum once more, Red." Jett says as he kisses her. Enzo places himself between her legs and begins to eat her pussy. I step up when she breaks her kiss with Jett and shoves my cock down her throat.

"Fuck!" I grunt. Jett stands up on his bed, his cock looking right at me. I lean forward and lick the pre-cum from his tip before taking him deep. Ria moans around my cock, making me do the same around Jett's.

"Damn, Rialynne, does seeing Kai take Jett's cock turn you on?" I hear Xander ask and soon I can feel her screaming another climax around my cock. I'm still at the back of her throat. Jett pulls out of my mouth. Ria moves up and kisses me. I taste myself as she tastes Jett.

"Xander, bed now." She orders him. He listens. She straddles him and then sinks down, her head falling back as she begins to fuck him.

"What now, my queen?" I ask, taking her breast in my mouth.

"Enzo, here." She points at her ass. He moves without question.

"Open your mouth, Ria." He sticks two fingers in her mouth, ensuring to coat them well. Jett brings a tube a lube over to him and Enzo smirks. Removing his fingers from her mouth, he coats them in lube. "You going to let me fuck that pussy before your ass?"

"Yes," she moans and Xander pulls out of her, pulling her down to expose her glistening pussy to us. Enzo steps up and thrusts inside her while running his fingers over her tight hole.

"Kai, Jett," we both move at the sound of her name. "Make each other cum." She orders and we both know what that means. I lay down next to Ria, as Jett moves on top of me. His mouth wraps around my cock as I take his. We suck each other and I hear Ria climax on Enzo from the sight of it.

If I had any doubt about being into guys, this right here changes it, because feeling the way Jett is working my cock is giving me dirty ideas.

"Are you ready for us?" Enzo asks and Jett and I both stop to look at her.

"Yes, but I need all of you." Jett gets off me and we stand up around her.

"Tell us how you want us, Red." Jett says as he moves in front of her.

"Xander and Enzo first, then you two." She says without shame. She moves to straddle Xander, taking him in her pussy while Enzo begins to enter her ass. She moans and they pick up a rhythm. Kissing her and flicking her nipples while fucking her.

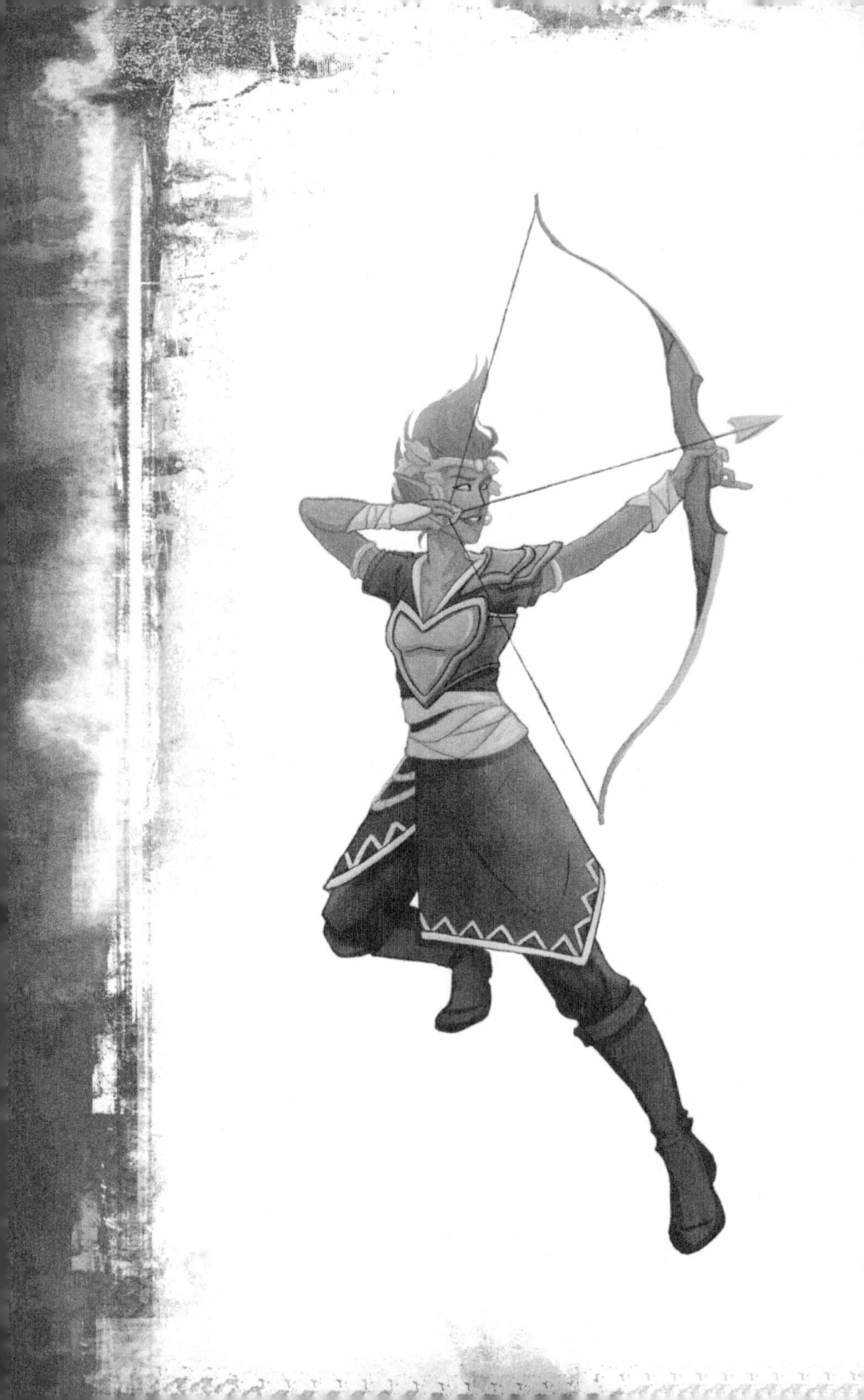

Chapter Eighteen

RIALYNNE

Enzo and Xander have me pinned between them. While Jett and Kai watch. I honestly cannot tell you how hot it is to watch these men do whatever to please me. The way Jett and Kai pleased each other turned me on more than I was before. Thinking about it as I watch them jerk each other, I clench down on the other two feeling my fourth orgasm surging through me. They soon follow.

None of us have time to recover as I am picked up, Jett thrusting inside my pussy while Kai claims my ass. I cry out in the pain and pleasure of it. They do not care that Xander and Enzo's cum was starting to seep out. They fuck me fast and hard until we were all spent and sated.

Our harem moved to Jett's shower and cleaned ourselves up. When we were dressed again, I laid my head on Kai's lap and my feet across Enzo's, as we sat around Jett's coffee table.

"I never thought I could be this happy." I say out loud. Kai smiles at me.

"You deserve to be happy, Ria. That is all we want for you." He leans down and kisses my forehead.

"School starts tomorrow, that means your training will begin. We will still collaborate with you in our secret spot, only we will need to modify it so we can train your other senses." Xander says.

"You mean my sight?" I ask.

"You have earth magic coursing through you, which means the earth can aid you. Once you are in tune with the way the vibrations feel, you will be able to feel everything around you." He explains.

"Do you honestly think I will be able to fight without this?" I ask, touching the golden band.

"That is the goal, because if you rely on it and it breaks again..." Xander swallows, as if he does not want to think about what could happen.

"Good. Now, how do we sneak her back out of here without getting seen?" Enzo asks.

"I am a rogue," Kai deadpans. "I can get her out of here without anyone seeing." I cannot believe I was afraid of him when I first saw him. It feels so long ago.

"Get her back to her room. We will see you tomorrow in class." Xander says as we all get to our feet. I kiss the others good-bye, my heart feeling complete.

Kai was right, the power of his order got me out of there in the blink of an eye. The sun was bright in the sky as I made my way from the main hall to the library. I want to see if there are any more books on Jada, or any other druids.

"Where have you been hiding, hermit?" Melody steps out from the columns with her two lackies.

"Have you been waiting for me?" I ask, crossing my arms over my chest.

"You haven't been at the house since that pitiful performance at try-outs, and I know you don't have a boyfriend." She does that stupid hair flip again.

"I don't have time for this." I tell her, moving past her, but her lackies block the doors.

"No, but you have time to fuck the kings." For a moment, I fear we got caught, but then I remember she is grasping at nothing.

"You'd like that wouldn't you?" She raises a brow. "Let me elaborate. You would enjoy finding out that the four kings chose a hermit whore over your entitled ass, because then you might learn some humility." I snarl. I take the taut look on her face as my opportunity to escape to the library. I was not looking for a fight, but when she threw a fireball at me, that was it.

Forming two fire swords in my hands, I turn and quickly notice she has a whip. "I'm tired of your shit, Melody."

"Come on then." We engage. Her whip wraps around my blades but I rip them free, using my own magic to bend her's to my will. My druid magic fuels me as we continue to clash, fire with fire. "Go back to wherever you came from, whore. We don't want you here."

"Make me." I growl as her whips form two blades of their own, and we continue our dance of flames. Each time our fire clashes, sparks form, and my other elements are begging for release. Without thought, I call on my air and blast her with a mix of fire and air.

"What?" Before she has a chance to recover, I take control of the fire magic inside her and lock it down. I quickly form chains of fire around her wrists, ankles, and neck. The fear on her face makes me feel powerful, and I launch a fist of air and fire at her face. Before it makes contact, I am pulled backwards.

"Back off, Red." Jett growls. "Fighting is not tolerated at the academy. Shall I give you detention?"

"Ask her. She just wouldn't stop. Ever since I got here, she has been a bitch to me. Instigating. Nagging. Insulting." I move closer, dropping my tone to a whisper. "I'm a fucking Queen, Jett. I don't deserve to be disrespected." Enzo helps her to her feet, and she wraps her pathetic arms around him.

"Thank you, my King. She just attacked me out of nowhere. You should expel her." She sobs and whimpers, making a growl resonate in my throat.

"You honestly think he is going to believe her over you?" Jett whispers in my ear. "Get back to your room and stay there. I will manage this." I look at him, he pushes me in the direction of my house.

The door slams as I stomp through the lobby. "Ria, where have you been?" Toni runs up and pulls me into a hug.

"I went to see my family." It is not a lie. A part of me feels as though the four kings have slowly become a family for me. I do not know what we are, but I know they bent the knee and devoted themselves to me. That must mean something.

"Oh, well I'm glad you're back. We have classes tomorrow, and you need to be rested because you made the team, and we practice every other day." Toni tells me excitedly.

"Great. Thanks Toni. I'm going to bed." I tell her. She walks me there, telling me about the night she and Damarias had. It was not as intense as my time with the four kings, but she seems happy.

"I don't know Ria, but I think I might have my first boyfriend."

"That's great Toni! I'm so happy for you both. Can we talk more tomorrow?"

"Of course, you get to sleep." I shut and lock my door, flopping down on my bed.

I moved my hand to my neck and realized my necklace was gone. "Fuck, where is it.?"

I look around my room and then it hits me, the only place it could be is on the field. I peek out and see Toni talking to one of the other students. I will have to wait until they are all asleep.

The hours tick by until I know the house is asleep. I slipped on an all-black outfit that I might have taken from Kai after our intense five-way- His seafoam scent still lingers on it. I creep down the steps, using my air magic to silence my footsteps. I make it out the front door and then run straight for the arena.

It is pitch black, so I use my fire to form a light in my hand. I walk through the corridor that leads straight onto the field but stop the moment I hear voices.

"Just like that." Not just any voices. Melody's, and it does not sound like she is talking. "Oh, Enzo! Fuck me good!"

This bitch. Fantasizing about my man. I douse my light and sneak out to get a good look. My heart breaks at the sight. Melody is on all fours, with Enzo fucking her the way he did me just last night. Rage, pain, and pure hatred swell inside me.

"What the fuck?" I yell and they freeze.

Enzo's eyes widen as he looks at me.

"Go away whore, my man and I are making love." Melody starts moving herself on him.

"Ria, I can explain." He says, pulling out of her.

"What? You do not need to explain anything to her. She's known from the start that you and I were dating." Melody says, while crawling in front of Enzo and taking his cock in her mouth. Bile rises in my throat at the thought of where it was before.

"Get off me." Enzo growls and pushes her aside.

"Don't." I tell him, before turning and running. But he catches me and pulls me back.

"Don't run from me. I can explain." I punch him so hard, my knuckles crack.

"Stay away from me. And don't you ever touch me again." I run so fast; my bones begin to crunch. A sob leaves my throat. I take off to the sky, not caring if anyone sees. I need to get away. Enzo, one of my kings, cut my heart. He betrayed me and for what? Another hole to fuck. I knew I was not good enough.

A burst of green flames leaves me as I internally scream with the pain of his treachery. *I should have never trusted them. Any of them. Kai and his gentle nature. Jett and his charming facade. But Xander, he was honest about his feelings from the beginning. They hate me, and will do anything to destroy me. But now the beasts have awoken, and I will destroy them all.*

After flying around, blowing off steam, I shift back into my naked elf form before landing on my windowsill. Another advantage of having my own room. I slide it open and slip inside. I am leaving this academy and finding the shadow rebels. If anyone will help me destroy the kings, it's them.

I grab the book on Jada and get dressed into the normal clothes I had on when I got here. Packing a bag, I slip it on my back and think about flying out of here, before remembering it would tear my bag. I slip out the windowsill, using my air magic to gently lower myself to the ground. I make my way down the path directly towards the Chow Hall and then cut across the yard and walk straight out the gates.

A feeling of regret hits me as thoughts fly through my head. Not seeing Toni again. The look of incredulity on Enzo's face as I punched him. Tears threaten, but I swallow that shit down, because there is no use crying over someone who was never really yours.

"Where are you going, Red?" I stop at the sound of Jett's voice.

"I'm not telling you." I take a step forward and he blocks my path.

"Enzo told us what happened."

"Which part? Him fucking Melody or my fists?" I ask, swallowing the bile at the image that floods my brain.

"All of it. And the part about you transfiguring."

"And what, you here to lecture me?"

"No. Where are you going, Red?" he asks me. All of his usual playfulness and aggression is gone, as if he is afraid of what I am going to say.

"I'm leaving."

"Then I'm coming with you."

"No." I shake my head as two tears escape.

"I'll follow you, regardless. Look at me." I do not meet his eye, and he grips my chin, some of that aggression returned. "Tell me how to make it better. Do you want me to kill him?"

"I don't care what you do. None of you are mine. I just need to leave. I need answers I can't find here, and I don't think I will last another day at this academy." I told him.

"It's only been a week, Red."

"Feels like a month." He is silent as he runs a hand down my arm. The feeling of him threatens to make me break for him. To give in to this connection. I step back, putting distance between us.

"Don't walk away from me, Red." He sounds hurt.

"You and the other kings don't need me. Have your freedom. I'm done." I run past him, using my air magic to help me pick up speed. I do not look back, I wait for him to stop me, but he does not, and my heart cracks even more. That confirms it. None of them really wanted me. Just my body.

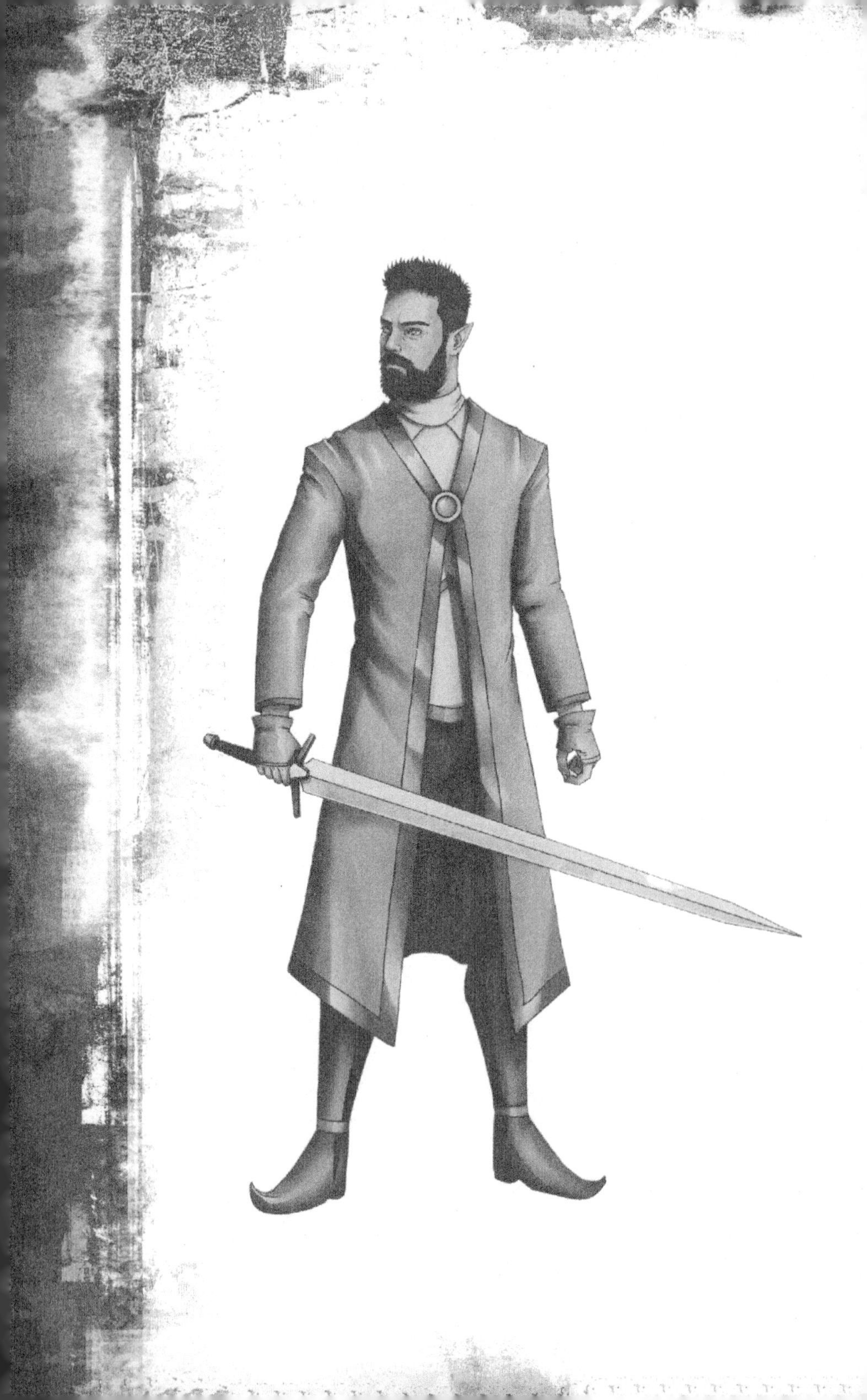

Chapter Nineteen

JETT

I chase after Red, even as she picks up speed. Fuck, she is fast. It must be her druid magic, aiding her speed. I won't stop until I know she is safe. I will not lose my mate. My queen.

My breathing picks up as I try to catch up to her, but she is gone. Like she disappeared into thin air, as if she summoned her own portal. I fall to my knees, impacting the hard ground as the ache of her distance tears me apart. She left me, and didn't look back.

Anger runs through me as I clench my fists and I feel my magic begging to explode. Getting to my feet, I turn back to the academy and run. I have one elf in my mind. A hunger to kill the person who hurt her. Made her feel like we didn't care for her.

I burst through the gates and sniffed out the clammy scent of my victim. I'm a warrior, not a simple hunter, my accuracy is unmatched. Her black hair comes into view as she walks out of Irfu stadium, a smug look stamped on her face, I pounce. My hand clamps around her slender neck, slamming her into the brick wall.

She screams, and I squeeze her throat tighter. Her nails dig into my skin as I feel her fire magic pushing against my air shield. I bare my fangs at her, letting her get a good look at the person who is bringing death to her.

"You made her leave. You hurt her with your desperate need for attention, and because of you, she is gone. Now, you die." I squeeze tighter, her lips beginning to turn blue. Her feet begin kicking.

"Let her go, Jett." Kai's calm tone comes from somewhere behind me.

"Red's gone and it's this bitch's fault." My grip tightens, and I know if I tighten more, her head will pop off. I feel his hand touch my shoulder, his seafoam scent washing over me. I've grown an attachment to him. We grew up together, but Kai and I formed a bond a long time ago. I was afraid the feelings we have for Ria might have changed it, but it has only strengthened it.

"We will get Ria back but killing this girl isn't going to do anything but bring unwanted attention to the school. To Ria." He says. I loosen my grip on Melody, pushing air into her lungs. Kai's soft hand goes to my cheek, and he turns me to look into his eyes. "I promise we will get her back."

I drop Melody and allow myself a moment of weakness to show. He is my best friend and we both know what we feel for her. What we feel for each other. There is nothing that could compare to this.

"I'm telling Enzo." Melody screeches, and tries to run off. Enzo steps out of the shadows blocking her. Next comes Xander. Soon we are surrounding her, all four of us glaring. "What is this, Enzo-bear?"

"I'm not your fucking 'Enzo-bear'. I'm a king. Get on your knees Bitch." He growls. I smirk at my cousin. She slowly lowers to the ground, her eyes glossed over with tears. "Lick our fucking boots." She whimpers, but does as he orders. When she is done, he signals for us to step back. "You will never speak of anything that has to do with us kings or

Ria again. Do you understand me?" she nods.

"If you so much as speak ill against her, or anyone else again, I will have you thrown in Vain Prison for the rest of your miserable life." I growl at her.

"Get the fuck out of here." Enzo barks. She scampers away like a whipped dog. In a different scenario, we would all be laughing, but we are all feeling Red's loss. Our queen left us thinking we don't care or need her.

"Where is she?" I ask. Looking to the three of them for an answer.

"We can track her magic, but it won't be easy." Xander says.

"She has no place to go. Do you think she went back to him?" I ask, dread itching at me. Would Red leave us to go back to Sarrs?

"I don't think she will go anywhere near him. But I wonder if she might go seek help elsewhere." Kai says.

"I think we should get some sleep. We don't need to raise suspicion on the first day of classes." Xander says.

"How will we explain her absences?" I ask.

"Quarantined in her room with an illness? I don't know, but Sarrs cannot have any reason to come here. You know he meets with the students who are considered troubled, or not committed. Ria's unexplained absence would be noticed." Xander says.

"Come on." Kai pats my back and I catch onto his gaze and nod. We all make it back to the faculty hall. Xander and Enzo go into their rooms, but I find myself following Kai into his.

"Can I stay here?" I ask him. I hate showing my weakness, but Red leaves me, me failing her, it's hitting me hard, and awakening things that I have had locked away since my parents died.

"Of course." Kai smiles. I strip out of my clothes down to just my boxers and he does the same. We lay down under the covers of his bed facing each other. I wonder why we haven't done this in a while. As kids we used to share a bed.

"What's on your mind?" he asks.

"A lot of things." I swipe a hand down my face. "I am stressed as fuck man. Red leaving, it hit me hard in a way that I haven't felt since our parents were killed."

"I know what you mean." He speaks. "Can I ask you something and you won't get pissed?" I nod. "Why are you okay with sharing her?" His question baffles me for a moment, because I wasn't okay with it. Until I saw how happy it made her. Then, when Kai and I did stuff for her pleasure, it was hot as fuck.

"I guess it's because I like making her happy." I shrug.

"Is that why you were okay sucking me off and letting me suck and kiss you?" he asks, and I look down at his lips again.

"Yes," I say. "And no."

"So, even without her here, you'd still kiss me again?" he asks, reaching out to touch my cheek.

"Yes." I answer. Our gaze intensifies as the space between us decreases and his lips brush across mine. He presses them together and I push him onto his back as I deepen our kiss, forcing my tongue between his lips. I feel myself hardening against his own erection.

I break our kiss and he swallows before I feel his hand tracing a line down my body. It sends a shiver down my spine.

"Do you want this?" he asks, and I nod my head. We kiss again and begin grinding against each other. It isn't enough. He flips us and begins to trail kisses down my body, pulling my boxers off before wrapping his mouth around my tip. My dick slides between his lips, a humming of pleasure coming from the back of his throat, making me instinctively thrusts forward. Pleasure ripples down my spine as I hit the back of his throat.

He begins bobbing up and down, licking and sucking, sending me into overdrive. But it still isn't enough.

I grip his hair and pull him backup to my mouth, tasting myself on him as we grind against each other.

I flip us over and then get off the bed, pulling out a bottle of lube from his drawer. He flips over without me asking and I climb on top of him. I run my hand up his spine before squirting some lube on my dick, rubbing it up and down, and putting some on his tight hole.

I have already had Ria this way, but this is different. This is my best friend, and solidifying this connection we have, only makes me wish she was here more. I put the lube down and line my tip up with his entrance and enter slowly. His back arches and he grunts.

"Fuck." I grunt, stopping when I am finally seated all the way inside him. Then I begin moving, fucking him hard. This is what we both wanted. What we needed to get the stress off our minds. I love Red with my entire soul. Fucking my best friend will never change that.

"Damn, Jett." I watch as Kai begins wanking himself off while I fuck him harder and faster, gripping his shoulders for leverage. With a final thrust, we are both coming and I fall on top of him. I pull out and then get up to get a towel for us.

"What do you think she is going to say when she finds out about this?" Kai asks.

"I think she will be dripping wet when we tell her. Besides," I pause pulling my boxers on. "You're my best friend, and we both have been bi for all our lives. We just haven't fucked another guy until tonight. I think we just needed to find the right one." I told him.

"Damn, that was almost sweet. Ria is apparently rubbing off on you." Kai says as I fall into the spot next to him. We are silent for a second. "This doesn't change the fact that she is my mate. My alpha didn't rise up when it met you."

"I know man. We can have fun. Besides, she gets off on watching us." I told him. He smiles.

"Good-night." He says and soon falls asleep. With my body relaxed I find sleep comes to me easily. Red's face appears before me one last time before my mind slips into the quiet abyss.

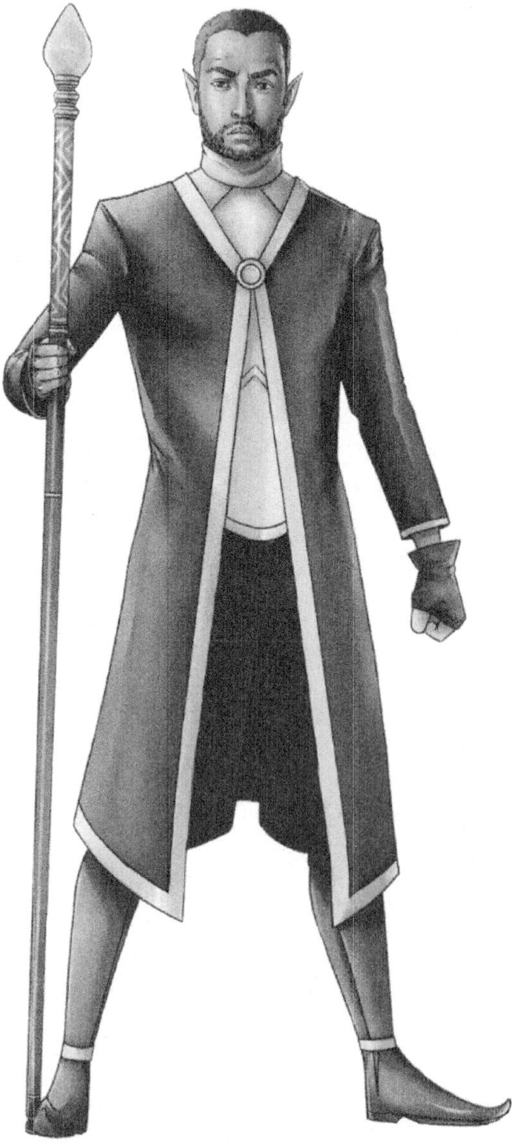

Chapter Twenty

XANDER

A loud exploding sound jerks me awake. Looking at the clock I note that the time is just past sunrise. Dressing quickly, I grab my stuff and rush out of my room, meeting the other three.

"What the fuck was that?" Jett asks. Bending down, I reach out with my magic, connecting with the roots of the earth. Chaos has erupted all over the school as a darkness engulfs it.

"We are under attack." I tell them. We spring into action, running out of the faculty hall until we reach the outside.

"Shadow rebels, why are they here? Is Roderick mad?" Jett asks.

"I don't think he is in charge of these ones." Enzo says. I suddenly begin to wonder who Roderick really is. Why is he so intent on us bringing Ria to him? Is he really her father? What if he means to use her? *Now isn't the time for these questions,* I think to myself as I watch the students fight for their lives.

"Save as many as you can." I tell the others, and we all break off to fight off the intruders. I dig my fingers into the earth and call forth my magic, feeling the vibrations of the nearest rebels. Cracking the ground beneath them, I watch as they fall inside the cavern I created, the students they were attacking are now running free.

A blast of fire bolts past me and I turn around, bringing an earth shield up just as more fire comes from two different elementals.

"You're going to have to try harder than that to bring me down." I yell. They charge forward with their swords. I form a rock sword in my left, moving my staff to my right hand, and prepare to fight them off. As their swords connect with mine, I use my mage magic to strengthen my hold.

"Where is the girl?" One of them growls through the mask he is wearing.

"What girl?" I ask as I push back with all my magic, knocking them back a few feet.

"The queen. Where is she?"

"There is no queen any longer. She died the night you all attacked." I tell them. Going with the story we created-instead of potentially lying. He charges for me again, but I don't let him get far as I slam my staff into the ground, causing a tremor that shakes the entire school. Some rebels don't hold their balance, falling on their backs, giving the students they were attacking the reprieve they needed.

A booming voice echoes through the entire grounds. Heightened by magic, Dean Ziba's voice resounds in my ears. "All of you will exit my school campus immediately, or you will all die a painful death."

"He is bluffing." One of the rebels' scoffs and begins to charge at the old man. I step up to stop him, but halt when I see Ziba raise a hand, lifting the rebel into the air. His hands go to his throat as the air is stolen from his lungs.

"You will not underestimate me." Ziba yells, and I can't help but feel pride and respect for the man. The rebels body goes limp. "I don't know what possessed you to attack innocents, but you will not be warned any second longer."

"Where the fuck is the queen?" One of them yells and I pray that no one has made a connection to Ria.

"There is no queen. I would know if there were one. We only have four kings." Ziba answers. They seem to believe him as portals start opening randomly everywhere. "All faculty meet me over here."

I make my way over to him, picking up students while on my way. Relief comes over me as I see the other three join me.

"Forgive me, my kings but I must be blatant with you." He says. I look at the others with a raised brow. "Is my Queen really dead? Or was she hiding here?" I open my mouth to answer but Ziba holds a hand up. "Never mind. The less I know the safer she will be. Now I need a count of the students. All injured will need to be seen by healers. If there are any fatalities, I need to know so I can alert families. I don't need to warn you that King Sarrs will probably be on his way, so get your stories straight." I knew what he was insinuating.

He suspected we knew about Rialynne, just didn't want to speak it out loud. I respect him even more for that. We disperse and spend the rest of the day tending to the wounded students. The school is in disarray and will take a while to rebuild.

"Hey, that was crazy," Jett says as he and the others walk up to me. I sip on some water.

"Yeah, how did they know she was here?" I ask.

"No clue. Maybe they suspected that she wasn't dead. I don't see how though. It's been over a month." Kai says with a shrug.

"I overheard Ziba talking with the other faculty members about closing the school down for the year. Half the student body was injured." Enzo comments.

"We need to get a handle on this before Sarrs shows up. If the rebels think she is still alive, there is no doubt he will think so too." I state.

"Isn't this a nice surprise." We all freeze in place as Sarrs deep voice booms from behind. Turning, I look at the regiment of guards stepping through the portal he must have come through. "Kneel before your king."

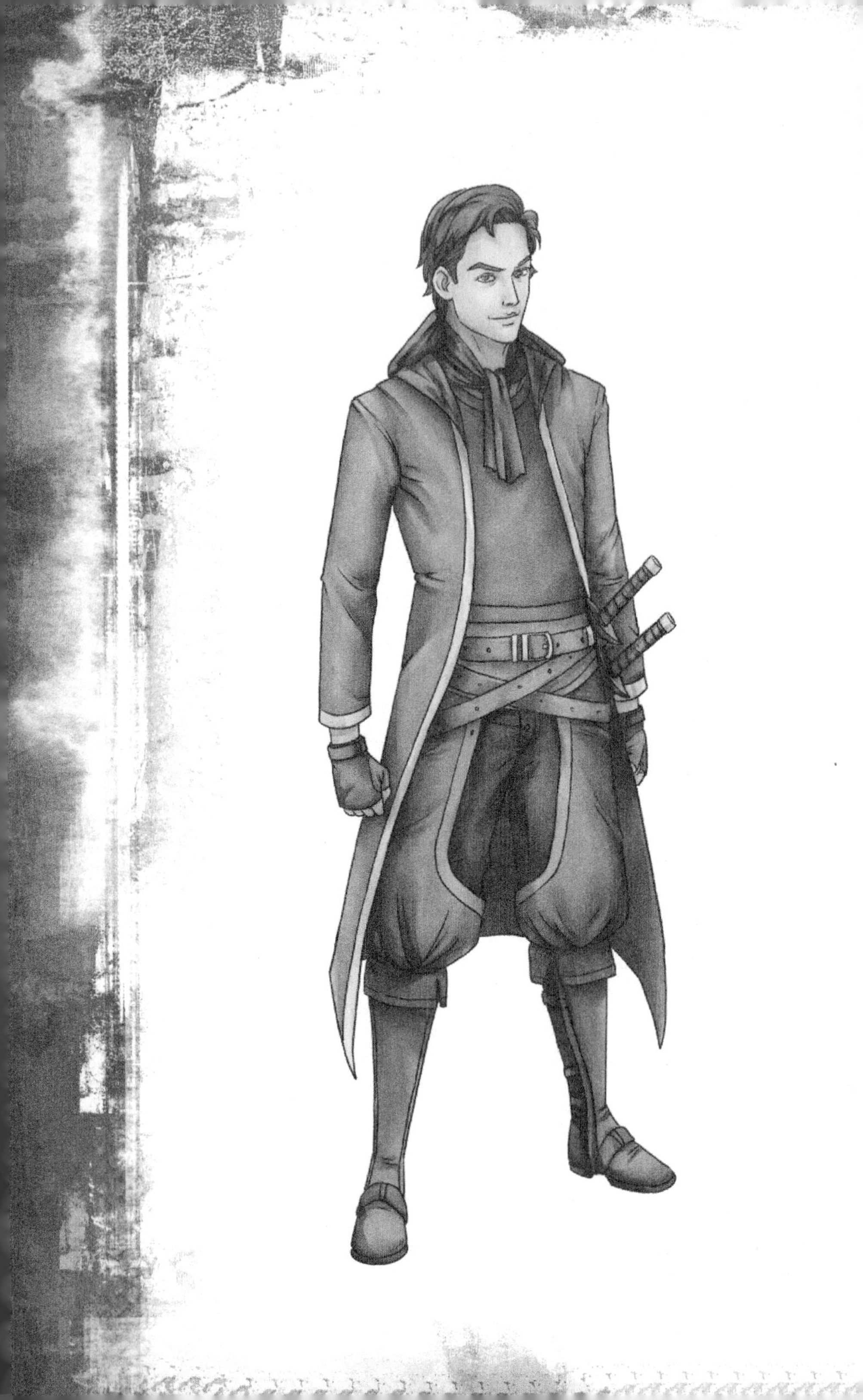

Chapter Twenty-One

ENZO

"I think it is time my fellow kings and I have a nice chat." Sarrs says, narrowing his eyes at us. "Seize all four of them in iron, make sure they are secured. Don't want them thinking they are free to use their magic against me."

"That isn't necessary, My King. We would never betray you." Xander says. Bile rises in my throat at the sound of him calling this vile creature a king. Sarrs smirks and nods.

"Very well. Xander, I knew your father. He was an honorable man so I will trust your word. If one of them steps out of line, I will kill you first." I gulp at that and exchange a glance with my cousin.

I stand shoulder to shoulder with Jett and Kai, Xander on the other side of Jett. We watch and wait to see what Sarrs is going to do as he looks around at the damage of the school.

"Why did the rebels attack a school full of innocent students?" he asks.

"They were looking for the deceased queen." Xander answers, keeping a stoic face.

"I see. Now, tell me something, Kai," His red eyes land on my friend. "Why do you think rebels would think the supposed dead queen is here? Alive and well."

"I don't know, My King. Perhaps they are as daft as they are disloyal?" Kai says. He hums and rubs his hands together before looking at Jett. Which is the last person he should want to piss off.

"Jett, you are the violent one of this group. Tell me, what motivates you to go after your victims?" I can hear a growl of warning forming in Jett's throat.

"Once I have heard of their whereabouts, I attack with all my strength, because if I have marked them, it's because they hurt what's mine. What's most important to me." I gasp at the clear devotion he feels towards Ria, and I wonder if that was meant for us as well? I know he and Kai have a special bond, and I would like to think that growing up together, plus our combined connection with Ria, has brought us all closer together.

"Good answer. Enzo," he moves to me. "Tell me the one thing that all kings hate most of all." I knew what he wanted to hear so I gave it to him.

"Disloyalty."

"That's right." He steps closer, his mouth brushing close to my ear. "Tell me why I am looking at the four most disloyal subjects in my entire kingdom?" I don't get a chance to answer as his fists hit my gut with a powerful thrust.

I cough as I taste copper in my mouth. He grips my hair, drags me forward and turns me to face the others.

"What are you doing?" Xander growls, Kai and Jett bare their teeth. Each has a ball of their element formed in their hands.

"Showing you what will happen if you lie to me again." He punches me in the ribs and I feel them crack. I wince in pain, but I don't give him my tears.

"He hasn't lied. None of us do. The queen died the night of the attack." Jett growls.

"I don't believe you." Another punch to the gut and he tosses me onto the ground before hammering a kick to my face, breaking my nose. "If you don't tell me where Rialynne is, your dear cousin is going to die."

My eyes catch onto Jett's dark blue ones, and I send him a pleading message not to betray her. If I am meant to die protecting her, I will. Rialynne Faith has brought out the real man that lies underneath my mask. I am a better man because of her. A better king, and a better friend. The four of us need her light and laughter to keep us from falling under the spell of Sarrs.

The only regret I have is the last time I saw her face, it was covered with hurt from supposed betrayal. Jett shakes his head, telling me not to give up. To fight for not just him, but her. I slowly get to my feet, spit my blood on the ground and raise two fire swords in front of me. Challenging Sarrs to a fight. The King growls and forms a sword of his own.

"You are a fool if you think I won't kill you boy." Sarrs growls, but I charge at him, swinging my fire against his. We clash and I can sense the power he has. It's almost too much for me to handle by myself. But I am not alone, not really.

The other three join, all of us attacking him from all angles. His guards swarm us as we fight for our lives. For Ria's life. Our Queen. As I am knocked on my back, Sarrs fire blade coming towards my neck, I thank Ares for bringing me Ria. The time I got to spend with her will stay with me even if I never get to see her again.

"I love you." I whisper before my eyes drift close, and I fall into darkness.

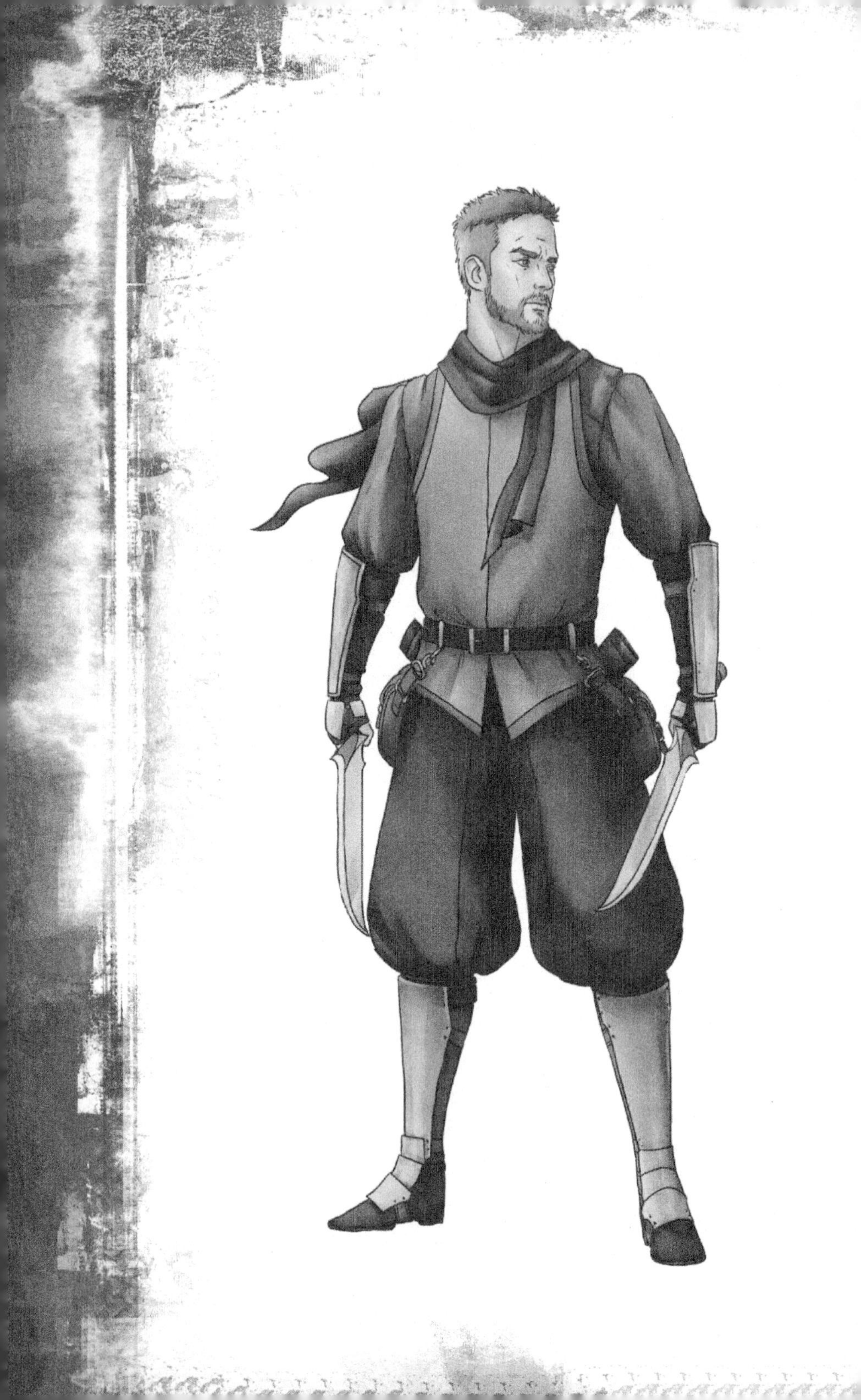

Chapter Twenty-Two

KAI

I blast another guard back with a wave of water magic, turning around just in time to see Enzo hit the ground hard. A crack resounds as his head impacts the ground. Blood begins to pool, and the fight starts to fade out of him.

"Not today." My world slows down as Sarrs brings his sword down on Enzo, I summon all the magic I have inside of me, forming the largest wave I have ever created. Aiming it at Sarrs, I let it all go with a war cry, knocking him back twenty feet.

My body goes limp as I fall to my knees and I crawl my way over to Enzo. Lifting his head in my lap, his sticky blood coats my fingers.

"Xander, portal us!" I yell. "Come Enzo, stay with us. Ria's going to kill me if I let you die." I tap his face, but he doesn't stir, Fear takes hold of me. "Xander!"

He rushes over with Jett, an air shield forming around us as the mage summons a portal and we are whisked away. We landed in the soft snow. The place where we all formed a bond with her. Our makeshift shelter is still in place. I carry Enzo inside and try to tap into my magic to try and heal him but there is nothing left.

"Guys, I'm tapped. One of you needs to heal him." I say looking at them.

"I can't do it. I need blood." Xander says and I can see how fatigued he is. I look at Jett.

"I need blood too." He says.

I offer my wrist. "Take some. You know what will happen if he dies."

Jett accepts my wrists, and I wince as his fangs pierce my wrist. Then it turns euphoric as the rush of endorphins hits me.

"Fuck." I groan, and I hate that this blood thing is a turn on, especially as it's not an appropriate time. Jett releases my wrists and begins to push healing magic into Enzo. The wound on the back of his head closes as the magic pulses through his body.

We lay Enzo on the couch before making our war over to the new addition Xander made after I gave him some blood too. Sitting at the table made from earth, I place my head in my hands.

"What do we do now?" I ask, my words muffled.

"We need to find her before he does." Xander says.

"How? We have no clue where she is? You said it would take time to track her down." I reply. He ponders before speaking.

"Then we don't track her. We track him."

"Who?"

"Sarrs." I raise my brows and he continues. "He has resources we do not. He is no doubt tracking her down as we speak. If we follow him, he will lead us to her."

"I am a rogue and so is Enzo, but how are you two going to get around unseen?" I ask, pointing at Xander and Jett, who is oddly quiet.

"Then you will just have to teach us how to be stealthy. Or, you two can track him, and once you get an idea on where he has tracked her to, just bring us with you." Xander says.

"I guess it's the best we have to go off of." I say with a shrug, hating that I both sound and feel defeated. "What about Roderick? Do you think he knows about all this?"

"I don't know, but I feel like we can no longer trust him. He wants Ria just as bad as Sarrs, and I can't help but think it isn't for a fatherly reunion." Xander says. I look over to Jett who seems to be lost in his own thoughts.

"You okay Jett?" His gaze snaps to me and he nods.

"I'm going to bed. Wake me if my cousin dies." He exits the room, and a moment later I hear his door slam shut. I wonder if I should go to him but decide it's best to leave him alone.

"I will begin tracking Sarrs tomorrow. Starting at the school, where his last magical signature is. I will need a way to get back. I don't have the ability to portal, so you will need to come with me." I tell Xander. He nods before speaking.

"Get some rest, man. I will watch over Enzo." I leave the kitchen. Dragging my feet up the stairs, I make my way into the bathroom, strip out of my clothes, and turn the shower on. The hot stream hits my back and I feel two arms wrap around me. Scenting air and snow wafted over me.

Turning around I hold Jett against me, giving him the comfort, he needs. We stay like that until the water runs cold. He dries us off with his air magic, and we dress. Together we climb into his bed, drifting asleep in each other's arms, letting the day fade away.

The next day, Xander and I step out onto the sandy landscape, I catch the scent of Sarrs magic and track it to the last spot he used it. A portal mark is embedded in the hard earth. I point at it and Xander uses his magic to portal to the location it took Sarrs.

On the other side, we find ourselves outside of the Cathedral. Hiding behind one of the houses, I crouch down in front of him and watch.

"I don't think he has left yet. We should come back every so often until I can pick up on a new signal again." I told him. As a rogue, I can track magic over time. Anytime a person leaves using magic, a signal tells me that they have left the area. It's difficult sometimes if there are other signatures blocking it, but Sarrs are distinct. Like death and blood.

"We should head back. At least, for now, I have his scent." Xander nods and summons a portal.

I spend the next couple months monitoring Sarrs movements while Enzo slowly recovers. Each time Xander and I portal back to the Cathedral, Sarr's signature hasn't moved.

"It's been four months. If he hasn't found her by now, then he never will." Jett says, as he reaches into the fridge for water. He and I have spent most nights together. Not being intimate as we once were. I think that was a one-time thing. Instead, we use each other for comfort.

"We will find her. With or without him I am beginning to think she may not be in Zavinia anymore." I replied.

"You don't think she would go there, do you?" Enzo asks.

"She could. I mean if she was desperate to get answers, she might have gone to the druid temple they have there." I mutter.

"It's a possibility." Xander ponders. Just like that, magic signals buzz in my head.

"It's time. Sarrs is on the move." I tell them to get to my feet.

"Where?" Xander asks.

"He is leaving Klestria," I close my eyes and follow the signature in my head. Not believing where it ends up. "He is past the borders. Into shadow rebel territory. To the fucking temple."

Without another word, Xander forms a portal, and we all step through. We run up the stone steps of the temple and bust through the doors. We hear them, Sarrs threatening her. Touching her. We try to break through, but a barrier is up. Even with all our combined powers it holds fasts.

"How the fuck is it still up?" Jett growls. A large growl erupts as a green dragon bursts through the top of the temple.

"There she is." Xander says.

"Let's go get our girl." I say with a smile. We are coming, my queen. We will never let you go again.

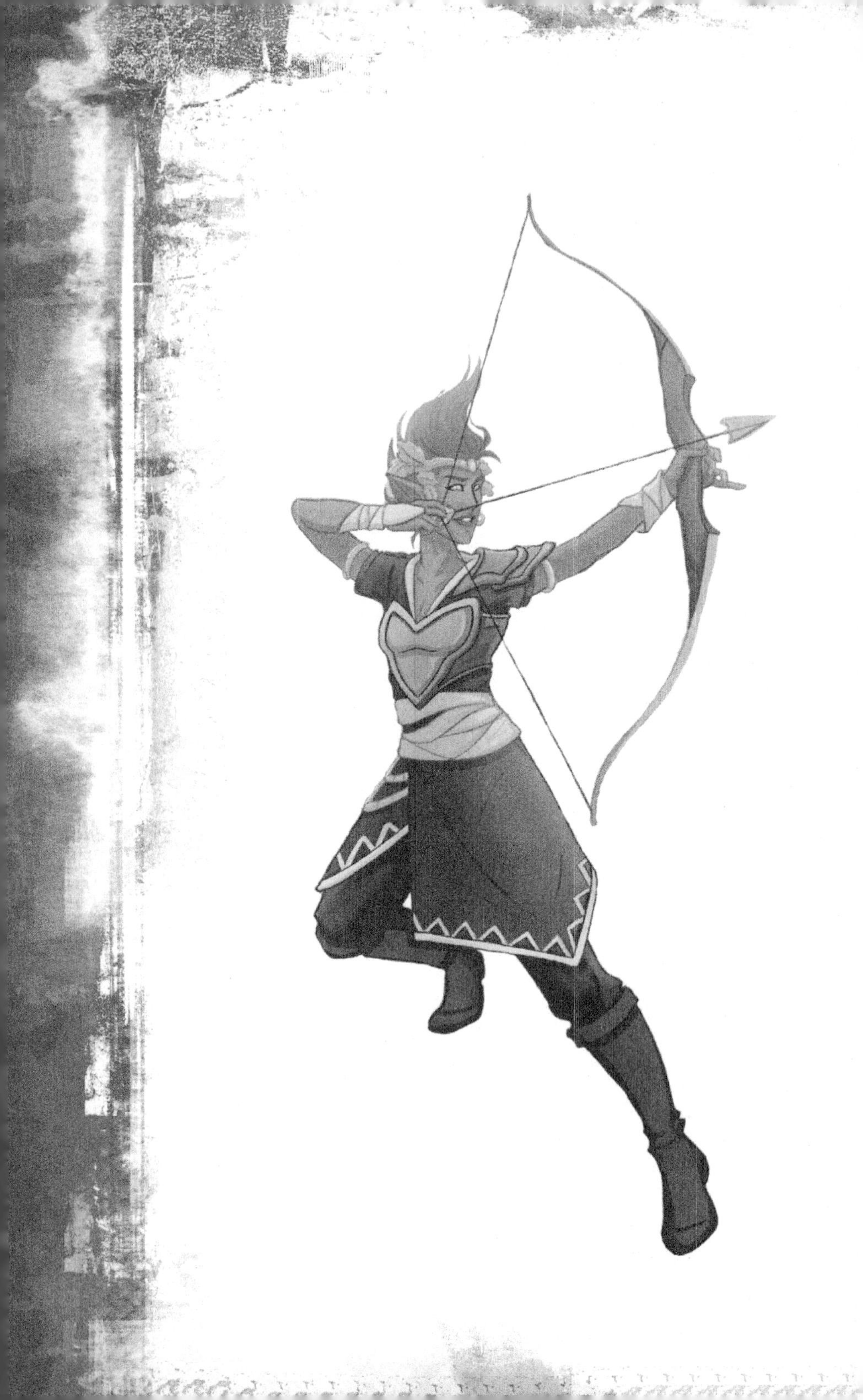

Chapter Twenty-Three

RIALYNNE

FOUR MONTHS LATER

I sit at the temple, looking at the words that I have slowly begun to understand. After running from the academy, I ended up past the border of the Avaniansphere, in shadow rebel territory. Dressed from head to toe in black, I was masked from wandering eyes with a glamor.

Jada's Temple was the first place I went, after hearing rumor of it back in the Oceaniansphere. I went to the village Toni grew up in to find out if any of them had heard anything about the druid.

"Jada was from here. She grew up here before she discovered she was an elite." An old fisherman told me as he cleaned some trout. "There is a rumor her temple is still standing."

"Where?" I asked.

"The territory beyond the border of the northern Territory. But I do not recommend going there. It means death for loyalists." I smiled, paying the man before making my journey here.

My butt starts to go numb from sitting on the pillow that surrounds the statue of Jada. I thought coming here would at least give me some sort of connection to her. To help me know what it means to be an elite druid. The only way I am going to take down the kings and destroy them is by mastering everything.

"Still nothing?" Monk Tilly asks. Monks service the temple. They are like the ladies of the Cathedral back in Klestria. Only they adorn themselves in long white robes, shave all the hair from their bodies, and take a vow of celibacy in service of Ares.

"Nope." I shrug.

"What is it you hope to learn from the past?" he asks as I get to my feet.

"I don't know. I just thought she might speak to me." None of the monks have paid me any attention. They do not know what or who I am. I have taken up residence here for two months.

"Try letting go of whatever is keeping you from reaching out to her." he says, and I sigh. I know what he means, even if he does not. The four kings broke something inside me that was starting to heal. All my anger and pain is eating me up.

"Thank you." I bow, and he leaves me alone again. I look at Jada's statue, posing with her bow and arrow, and resting my hand on the bow, I close my eyes and will myself to let go. My fingers feel the smooth stone as I push my druid magic into it. Calling onto the spirit of her.

"Let go of the pain." A female's voice radiates through my mind.

"Jada?" I question. I sense power pushing against mine. "You're here!" Suddenly the connection snaps and I am knocked off my feet. "What the fuck was that?"

"Did you think you would get away from me?" My throat dries as Sarr's familiar voice echoes in the hall. "You look good for a dead girl." He steps out from behind the columns, and I am not sure what to do.

"How did you find me? This is shadow rebel territory." He smirks at me. A regiment of guards runs into the hall.

"A little bird told me you were here. Did you think I couldn't manage a few rebels?" He steps towards me. His red eyes narrowed at me. "Why did you run away from me?"

"I didn't." I said, hating the fear coating my voice.

"You've been gone for months, Rialynne. I know you have not been here all this time." I shook my head. "Where did the four kings hide you?"

"They didn't." I spoke. Only able to form two-word sentences. His large hand brushes my cheek, and he smirks. A resounding sound echoes across the hall as his hand slaps my face.

"Don't lie to me, pet. Did you spread your legs for them?" He growls, before gripping my throat and lifting me off the floor. "Are you a full woman now?"

"No. Stop." He pushes me against the wall. I look around for someone to help but there is no one. *You do not need anyone. You are an elite druid, kick his fucking ass.* Sarrs rips my leggings off me, and I scream as he cups my pussy, inserting a finger. I scratch and claw. "Stop it!"

"No. If you can open yourself to them, you can open yourself to me." I scream again, tears flooding down my face as he reaches for his pants and pulls them down releasing his cock. "You're going to be a good little girl and take me, or I will kill you."

The way he says 'good girl' has me wanting to vomit, opposite meaning to the times Jett said it. He finally removes his finger, turning me around and forcing me under him. *I will not be raped.* I call on all my power, and just as he places his tip at my entrance, my body erupts into my green dragon form.

Sarrs is knocked twenty feet from me, and uses his air magic to stop himself from hitting the wall. "Impossible." He growls.

I shoot fire at him, and he dodges it. The palace guards ready themselves to attack. "Capture her. I want her alive." Sarrs commands.

I growl and then release my fire again. They back away long enough for me to make my exit. As soon as the roof bursts open, I take to the sky.

Putting distance between myself and the man who just assaulted me. I am no longer safe in this world. A scream erupts from my throat as my emotions take over.

My vision begins fading as my power slowly drains from my body. *I am falling into darkness. It consumes me. Ares calls for my soul as I hit the earth and feel my body shatter.* A light surrounds me, and I look down and see myself in all white. I touch my head and feel my headband is gone. Examining my surroundings, I notice there is nothing around for miles and I realize I must be in the realm of Ares.

"Welcome, Rialynne of Klestria." I turn around and see her. Jada, the last elite druid.

"Am I dead?"

"Not yet. There are four men desperately trying to keep you alive." What? She could not mean who I think. "I know you have been calling me for some time, but I couldn't reach you. Not until now."

"You mean with a near death experience or after I was assaulted by the man who raised me?" she sighs.

"After you claimed your power." I realize that I can hear her. "And you destroyed that ghastly device."

"How can I hear you?"

"Because Rialynne, you don't need a magical hearing aid. You can hear when you want to. Being deaf is not a disadvantage. If anything, it gives you an upper hand."

"How?"

"You don't need to rely on it. Your other senses become sharper. Just as your mage king told you. Using your earth magic will allow you to feel everything before anyone could ever hear it."

"Have you been watching over me?" Jada smiles.

"You are my descendant. Of course, I have. The first true elite druid since my time." I see pride cross her features.

"What do I do now? Sarrs and the rebels will be after me." I sigh.

"You fight. Tell me who you are." She puts a hand on my cheek, and

I feel familiarity in her touch.

"My name is Rialynne Faith." I answer.

"No, the real you. I want everyone to know who you are." I sigh. "Never doubt yourself."

"My name is Rialynne Faith, and I am the Queen of Klestria. The first true elite druid in centuries."

"Good. Now own it." I take in a deep breath closing my eyes and scream at the top of my lungs. My eyes flutter open and I sit up.

"She's awake." Xander exclaims, sounding relieved.

I glance around, and I see them.

"Ria?" Kai looks at me. All four kings keep their distance.

"Red?" I look at Jett. Then Xander. My throat stops as I meet Enzo's eyes. I cannot help the fire ball that I toss at his stupid head.

"Guess that means you're still pissed." Xander states. I get to my feet and scowl at them before looking around. It looks like we are back in the shelter we made the first time I met them.

"Why did you bring me here?" I ask.

"Because it's warded against Sarrs and the rebels." Kai answers. The sound of his name causes a shudder down my spine. Jett notices, narrowing his eyes at me.

"What happened at the temple?" He asks.

"Nothing I couldn't manage." I told him.

"Don't lie to me, Red."

"Don't call me that." I snarl, squaring up to him.

"No, you are Red. *My Red.* Whether you like it or not. You belong to me."

"I belong to no one." I whisper. I cannot seem to get the feeling of Sarrs touch off me. I turn away to hide my shame. I should have fought him the moment he made his intentions known. I was weak.

"Ria…" Kai steps forward but I step away from him.

"Don't touch me." I snap. "I don't want to be touched. Just tell me how you found me. And who dressed me." I look down and see the all-white outfit I was wearing when I met Jada.

"The day after you left the academy, there was a rebel attack." I gasped, instantly thinking of Toni and Damarias. "Your friends are fine. But the school took a hit. Classes are canceled for the year." Kai continues. "The rebels were there for you. Not sure how they found out that you were alive and that you were there. Did not get a chance to find out. Once they realized you were not there, they left."

"Did anyone die?" I would feel ashamed if someone died because of me.

"No, just some injuries that the healers managed. It didn't seem like it was a planned decimation." He explains.

"Right because they just wanted to kidnap me and take me to their leader." I sigh. "What else?" I urge Kai.

"After the attack, Sarrs showed up and basically tried to beat the shit out of us. He obviously didn't succeed and the four of us went into hiding after that." I put my hand to my mouth, not wanting to believe him. "We wouldn't tell him anything about you or confirm that you were still alive."

"You betrayed him, to protect me?" I got to my feet, trying to make sense of it.

"We knelt before you and devoted ourselves to you." Kai states. "Our loyalty belongs to you, our queen."

"No, it doesn't." I cannot glance at Enzo. Not without revisiting what I saw that night. "How did you find me?"

"We kept an eye on Sarrs movements and when we sensed him moving, we knew it was because he located you. We followed him." He paused, waiting to see if I would interject. "We tried to get to you before him, but we were too late."

"When did you show up?" I did not want to look at him. It would be too humiliating if they saw what he did to me.

"When…" his voice cracked. That told me enough. "I'm so sorry Ria. There was a magical barrier keeping us out. Xander could not fight it. We don't know what kind of magic he was using but we couldn't get to you."

"So, you saw. You watched him and did nothing." I was yelling, angry not at them but at myself.

"He is going to die for ever daring to touch what is ours." Jett growls.

"I don't belong to you. Don't you understand that? Whatever we were is gone. I do not want anything to do with any of you. You should not have come for me. You should've let me die." I sink to the floor.

"No, Red." Jett pulls me into his lap. "You are mine and I am yours. We did not get to you, but you saved yourself. We watched you fight him and take your true form, and by the goddess, it was mesmerizing."

I stare into his dark pools of blue and find pride and admiration reflecting in them. "I'm sorry, Red."

"We all are." Xander finally speaks and I feel his eyes on me. "Tell us how to help you, beautiful."

"Just be with me." I say as I bury my face into Jett's chest, breathing in his airy scent. I must have fallen asleep at some point because I wake to find myself tucked in bed with Jett's arms wrapped around me. I take in his peaceful features, memorizing them once again.

Wiggling out of his arms, I exit the room and make my way downstairs. "Escaping again?"

Enzo.

I ignore him and walk to the new edition they made-A small kitchenette. I pour myself a glass of water. "How long are you going to ignore me for?"

I do not answer as I place my glass down and walk past him. He grabs me and pulls me to him. I push him off me and growl. "You hate me. You hate me for fucking Melody. Fine. Hate me. But don't act like you don't still want me."

"I do hate you. You betrayed me. Betrayed my trust."

"If you would just let me explain what happened…"

"I saw what happened." I interrupt. "Don't remind me or else you won't breathe a second longer." Enzo's eyes alight with the flames of his magic. My breathing increases as I sense the hate between us increasing. As much as I hate him, the need to feel something other than the pain Sarrs caused me overpowers it. In a moment of weakness, I pull him down and crash my lips to his. It is not gentle as I unleashed all my hate for him, pushing it into the kiss. He returns it ten-fold.

Pushing me against the back wall and he tears my clothes from me before, incinerating his own. "You want to hate me, fine. But I'm going to remind you why you love taking my cock." He thrusts inside me as I moan his name. I scratch at his back as his thrusts speed up. His hand finds my clit as his mouth finds my nipple.

"Enzo, make it go away." I moan, and he growls.

"You want me to make you feel good?" I moan my answer and kiss him again, biting his lip. I feel my orgasm coming. It has been too fucking long. I clench down on his cock as I scream my releases and he growls' his. I look into his bright eyes and feel all my hate gone, the memory of Sarrs completely washed away by the intensity of this moment.

"I love you, Ria." I gasp at the three words, I have never heard spoken to me from anyone besides from my parents. "I would never betray you. I know you thought I did but what you saw was an illusion of me. Melody thought it was the real me, but it was not. I did it to shut her up."

"What?" I say, shaking my head.

"Xander casted the spell. Somehow Melody found out that we were all in a relationship and she was going to go to the Dean and out us. I offered her the one thing she was begging for."

"Enzo, you did that? For me?"

"I love you; I should've said it sooner but the moment I saw you walk through those ball room doors, my soul recognized you. You're my soul mate Rialynne Faith." He kisses me hard.

"Enzo, I'm sorry I didn't listen to you."

"I should've told you the plan, but I wasn't expecting you to walk out on that field. What were you doing there anyways?"

"I lost my necklace." I sigh, my face falling with the emotion.

"We'll find it. I promise." I kiss him again and feel him hardened inside me.

"This time, I am making love to you." I kiss him as he walks us backwards, laying me on the cushions. It is slow and full of passion. I feel his love for me radiating inside me, and for the first time in a long time, I feel like I am home.

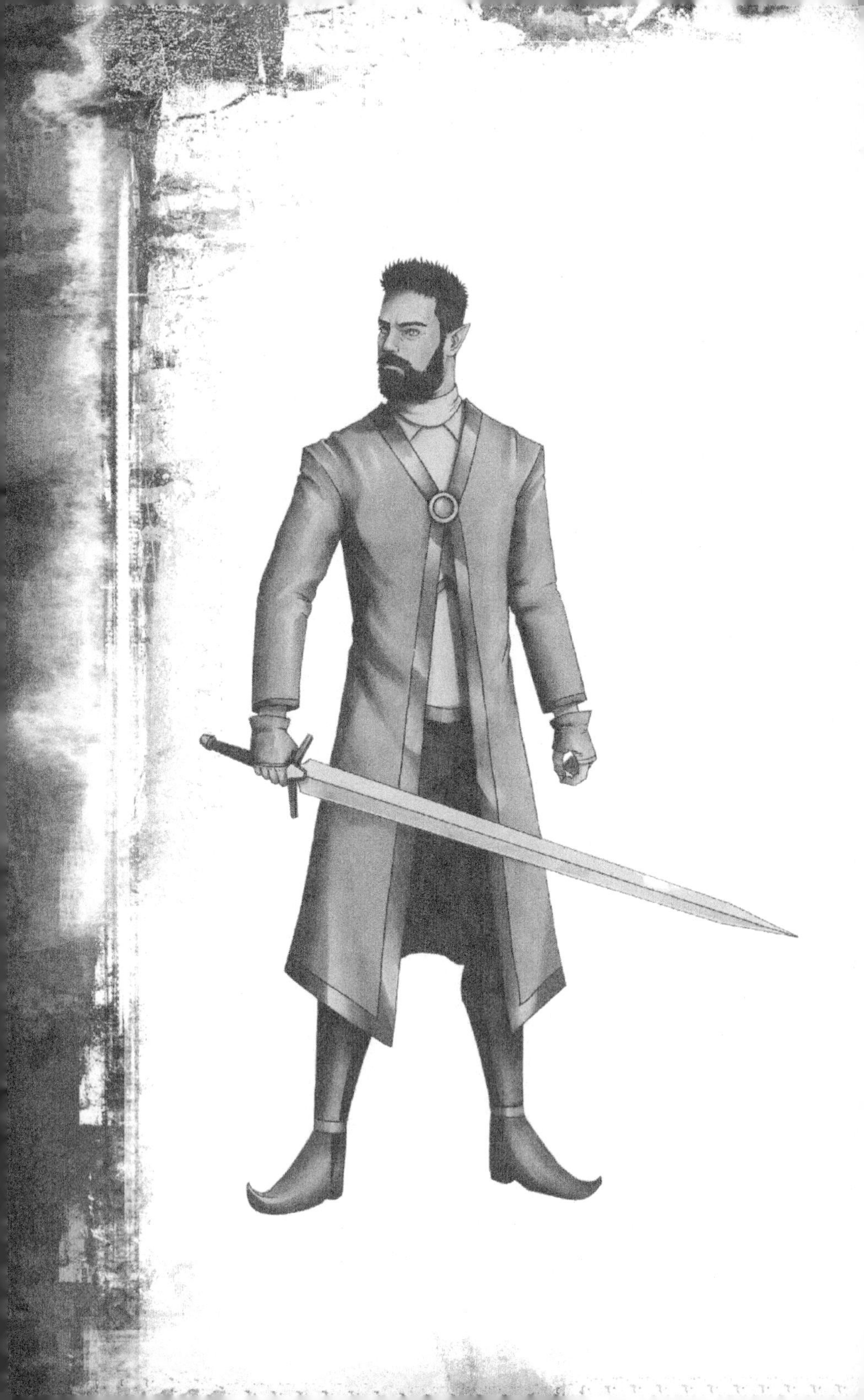

Chapter Twenty-Four

JETT

I wake up alone in my bed and instantly start to freak out. It is new for me, because I do not do that.

"Red?"

Shoving the covers off me, I rush down the hall to her room and see it's vacant. I check Xander's, then Kai's, waking them up in the process.

"What the fuck dude?" Kai growls.

"She's gone. Again."

"Fuck." Xander says, and we all rush down the steps. We freeze as we see her lying naked on the couch in Enzo's arms.

"I guess they worked through their shit." Kai says.

"Thank Ares, because we can't have our family broken." I say, shocking them both. "What? Red needs all four of us just as much as we need her."

"Tell me how you really feel." She sleepily murmurs.

"How about I show you." I say with a smile, approaching her. She turns over, her back pressed to Enzo's chest and I lean down and kiss her. I move my hand to her dripping pussy. "Were you dreaming about me?"

"Yes." She moans and arches into my touch.

"Ready for round three." Enzo growls, before thrusting inside her.

"Enzo." she moans, as the other two join us. We all strip bare as Enzo slowly fucks her, bringing her to her first climax.

"It's time to show our queen what it means to be worshiped by four kings." I state, and we all approach her. As she climaxes, I shove my cock in her mouth, muffling her scream as I pound into it. "Good girl."

"Fuck, Ria you're so beautiful." Enzo grunts as he picks up his pace. She takes me deep and chokes. Her fangs pierce my skin and I am still inside her, letting her drink from me.

"Kai, come here." I command. He comes without protest, and crashes his mouth to mine as I take his cock in my hand. We have been doing our own thing since Red left. When I break our kiss, my eyes land on Red's, they are filled with lust. "You like watching us?"

She nods around my cock. I smile then pull my cock from her mouth. I pull Kai towards me and kiss him, our shafts rubbing against each other. "Xander, I want your cock in my mouth." Red commands.

Xander moves forward and begins fucking her mouth. Kai breaks our kiss and watches as Enzo cums' inside our girl. "What do you want, Red?" He asks.

Xander steps back allowing her to speak. She gets up and moves between the three of us, kissing us deeply before pushing me onto my back. She straddles me, then pulls Kai behind her. We give her what she wants, Kai entering her ass, as I feel her pussy clench around me. She takes Xander in her mouth again.

We fuck her into another climax. Xander spurts in her mouth, and she swallows. He steps back, taking a seat next to Enzo, watching us fuck her. I kissed her, not caring that Xander's cum was still coating her mouth.

"Kai, Jett," she moans. I love that sound.

"What do you need, Red?"

"You." My heart clenches and all my self-restraint crumbles as I cum inside her. Kai follows.

"Have you and Kai been fucking without me?" she asks, and we both laugh.

"Would you be pissed if I said yes?" I answered her.

"No, but I'm watching next time. Then joining." She says and we all laugh. This is what we needed. To reform our bond with her, and show her we still worship her. I haven't told her how I truly feel for her, but I know she knows it. Or at least I hope she does.

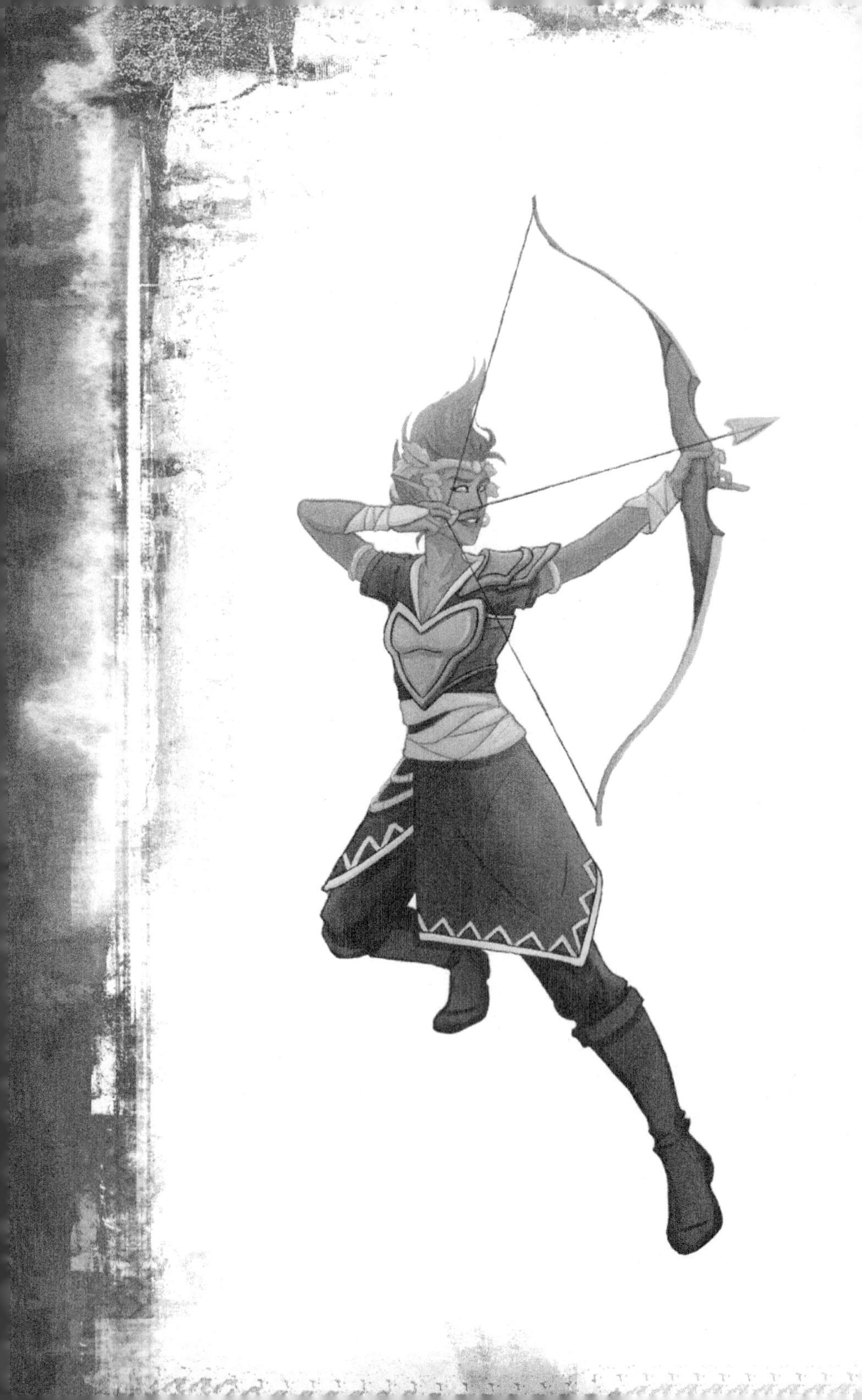

Chapter Twenty-Five

RIALYNNE

"You let yourself think the fight was over. I needed to remind you that it was not." He smirks. It has been a week since I escaped the temple and reconciled with my kings. Every day, I train with each element, for an hour without my headband on. It seems to be getting easier the more I practice it.

"Focus, Ria." Xander scolds, I can't hear him, but I see the way his mouth forms the words as I feel the intense energy radiating from him deep into the roots of the earth.

My vision is blocked out by the blindfold wrapped around my eyes. The kings decided it would help me better understand what it means to connect with the earth. My bare feet connect with the snow-covered ground as I find my center and focus.

A whooshing sound revibrates from my right side. Using my air magic, I form a shield and feel the rock bounce off it. I do not get a break between assaults as attacks come from all angles. I use all my elements to fight against the others. Air against earth, water against fire, fire against air, and earth against fire.

I am panting and sweating by the end. Reaching up, I pull the wrap from around my eyes and blink in the bright sun. When my eyes adjust, I see the aftermath of my powers. Melted spots litter the ground, shattered remains of earth cover various spots. A smile forms on my face at my work.

Until a fist connects with my rips. I double-over and find Xander smirking at me. "Pay. Attention." He mouths before handing me back my headband. I pull it on, sliding the prongs into their spot. It used to hurt, but it doesn't anymore.

"Did you have to punch me so hard?" I growl, as I push healing magic into me.

"You let yourself think the fight was over. I needed to remind you that it was not." He smirks before handing me a waterskin. I take it and gulp down the blood. I miss feeding from the vein, but it was agreed that I was becoming too reliant, and if I was not set on becoming blood bonded, I needed to stop.

"You did excellent, Ria. Another month and you won't need that anymore." He says pointing at the golden band attached to my head.

"I hope so. Then we can take on Sarrs." I speak.

"Ria, we are going to need an army to fight him. All five of us have been outcasted and labeled as traitors to the crown."

"What about the shadow rebels? They hate Sarrs. Perhaps we could convince them to be loyal to us?" I suggest. He sighs.

"I think we need to have this conversation with the others." I eye him, getting the feeling they have already discussed this scenario.

"Okay, let's go then." I start walking towards the shelter.

"Wait." He says and I look at him. He smiles then pulls me into a kiss. Not aggressive like Jett, but a soft one. "I wanted to have you once more before the others are around to steal you away."

"You have me Xander. As long as you want me." I say, cupping his face and kissing him again. We break away before walking hand in hand back inside.

The smell of smoked ham and potatoes makes my stomach growl with hunger. I watch as the other king works to set the round wood table. My eyes fall on Jett standing over the stove, flipping some ham.

I cannot help myself from walking away from Xander, to wrap my arms around Jett. "Hey Red, are you hungry?"

"Starving." I say, before walking over to my other two kings, and embracing them. As we sit down around the table, I smile at the feeling of sitting around the same table as our own family. My hand goes up to my neck, and sadness creeps in when I realize my necklace is still gone.

"Red?" Jett gives me a questioning look.

"My necklace, it's still gone. I used to touch it to feel close to Master Runk." I admit.

"Will you tell us more about him?" Kai asks, placing a hand over mine.

"He was there the day the assassins showed up. When I woke up, unable to hear, he figured it out and then crafted the device for me. As an earth elemental, he could do it. Once I fully recovered from everything, he was assigned to guard me by Sarrs." A tear escapes at the memory of him. "I told him I didn't want to feel weak and helpless ever again. We went to Sarrs to ask for permission for me to train, but we were denied."

I smiled at the next part. "Master Runk said 'fuck that' and we started training in secret. I worked so hard, every day for ten years. Then, out of nowhere, another rogue assassin attacked us during a training session. No one knew of our location except my ladies, and they had taken a vow to never betray me. I do not know how the rebels found us, but he died saving my life. I only got one arrow in before the guards rushed in and killed him." I start to cry again, but hold it back to finish my story.

"Sarrs was furious, and told me this is what happens when I disobeyed him. I was locked away in the Cathedral for the next twelve years. I worked in my room, and when I could sneak out at night, it was not the same. Master Runk gave that necklace to me on my sixteenth birthday. It was the only thing I ever had from him, besides this." I reach up, touch my headband.

"He will be honored forever." Kai says, before wiping my tears. "He saved the life of our queen. There is no cause greater than that."

"No one should die for me." I croak. "I don't want that, nor do I condone it."

"You don't have a choice, Red. Any of us would take a dagger to the heart if it meant saving you. You are the light this world needs." I sob, and am hit with anger at the thought of any of them dying.

"You are not allowed to die. None of you." I growl through my tears. "That is an order."

They all smile, shaking their heads. "That will be an order all of us will gladly disobey for you, beautiful." Xander says.

"Why?" I hate how weak I sound. I thought I was past all this self-loathing bullshit.

"You're our mate." Jett exclaims.

"You're our queen." Enzo says as he gets down on one knee.

"You're our heart." Kai says, kneeling next to Enzo. The last time they did this was before I left the academy.

"You're the reason we draw breath every day. The last thing we think about before we sleep and the first when we awake." Xander says, lining up next to the other three. I cup my mouth, my other to cover my beating heart.

"We love you, Red. I am undeniably and irrevocably in love with you." Jett's confession surprised me. I know Enzo said it, but I did not expect it from the others.

"I am in love with you Ria. My soul recognized you the moment you walked into that ball room. I know I am not a blood elf like Xander and Jett, but my heart and my soul knows you are my mate. I still want to marry you." Kai confesses. I am frozen in place.

"You already know how I feel, Ria." Enzo says with a wink.

"I don't know what to say." I tell them. They all laugh. "I don't deserve any of you."

"You deserve everything we have to give. If that means our death, then so be it." Xander says. I rise from my seat to kneel in front of them.

"Then I will give you my death in return. My heart and soul belong to the four kings of Zavinia and no one else." They all move at once, pulling me into their own kisses, each claiming me in their own way.

We laugh and form a group hug before breaking apart. My stomach growls, and we all sit down to continue our lunch. I know more must happen for a mating bond to truly be recognized. For blood elfs it can be blood sharing, but I have doubts they are willing to commit to me fully, so I do not bring it up. What they just gave me is enough.

Lying on the roof of our makeshift shelter, I stare at the stars, and wish to see Jada or Master Runk again. Nothing happens so I sigh and close my eyes, relishing the peacefulness that I feel up here. A break from the others, my own space.

"Master, I'm sorry I lost my necklace. I think you would be proud of me. I have come a long way in my skills. If you are watching over me, then maybe you would encourage me to continue to practice fighting without my headband on." I sigh, pulling it off and running my hand over the cold golden metal. "This is the last thing I have from you. I don't know if I will be able to let it go completely because I don't know how to let you go."

I feel something around me, and I turn around to see Xander waving to the spot next to me. I nod before putting my band back on. "Master Runk sounds like he was more than just a guard." He says.

"He was more like a father." I admit, and Xander wraps an arm around me. I lean my head on his shoulder, seeking out his comfort.

"My dad is sick." I snapped my head back, surprised that he shared this with me.

"How bad is it?"

"Blood poison."

"Shit. I'm sorry, Xan." He smiles weakly.

"I don't know how long he has left. I haven't been able to go home since we were exiled." Guilt washes over me, and he must realize it because he cups my face, staring at me. "Don't you dare blame yourself, beautiful. I do not regret a damn thing I have done for you. If I have any regrets, it is pushing you away because I was a coward. Falling for you scared the hell out of me but I don't regret it, because you're my fucking mate."

I press my lips to his, deepening it with my tongue before pushing him onto his back and straddling him.

"Mine." He growls before pulling me into another kiss. He hardens beneath me, but I just want to hear more about his father.

"As much as I want you right now, I want to hear more about your dad. How long has he been sick?"

"A little over a year. Someone breached and poisoned his blood supply. I still have not been able to figure out who. But the last time I spoke with his healer she said they were getting close." He wipes a hand down his face before sitting up. "He wants to meet you."

"You told him about me?" I smile.

"Of course, I did. You drive me fucking crazy." He smiles and I kiss him again. "I want you to meet him, Ria. I want to introduce you as my mate and my queen. Can I do that?"

"Of course." I smile, drawing him back into a kiss. I want to tell him that I love him, but something is pulling at my gut. A fear that this is not real. That having four mates is not possible.

Instead, keep it inside my head. *I love you Xander Zain.* I look into his dark eyes and see a flash of green pass over them before an air shield of warmth forms around us. I reach the hem of my tunic and pull it over my head. I have not had Xander alone, and I want him. Just him, in this moment.

A growl of possessiveness resonates in his chest before he leans down a clamp his mouth around my right breast, making me arch into his touch. I feel his fangs scraping against my skin and I want him to bite me. I need him to taste me.

"Bite me, please." He lifts his mouth. His eyes are glazed over with lust.

"Are you sure?" I nod and he kisses me on my mouth before trailing kisses down my neck, collar bone, and in between my breasts, he takes the left one and pierces my flesh, groaning with the taste of my blood. I rub my pussy over his erection trying to gain some friction. My undergarments are soaked with my arousal.

"I want you." I tell him and he pulls up, licking his lips before crashing them to mine.

I open my mouth, our tongues curling together. His hands move to my leggings, and he pulls them off me. We break our kiss so he can stand and remove his clothes. He sits back in front of me, and I move to straddle him, sinking down on him, both of us groaned with the movement.

"Make love to me, Xan." I cup his face and pull him into a kiss. He flips us over and begins a slow passionate pace. He picks up the pace as we get closer to our releases and in that moment, it clicks in place. I look into the depths of his eyes seeing the reflection of my green light cast over them.

"My mate." He growls.

"My mate." I repeat to him, and kiss him until we fall asleep in each other's arms on the roof. My soul has bonded with Xander, and I am saddened by the fact that it might not do the same with the others.

I wake up and look down at my right wrists, I see a tattoo of a mage staff wrapped around my wrists. Mark of the mating bond I share with Xander. I look upon his and notice a dragon has formed on his. My favorite animal and chosen transfiguration. My heart smiles as I look upon my mate.

"I love you Xander Zain." I whisper before kissing his cheek and curling myself back into his body.

My mate.

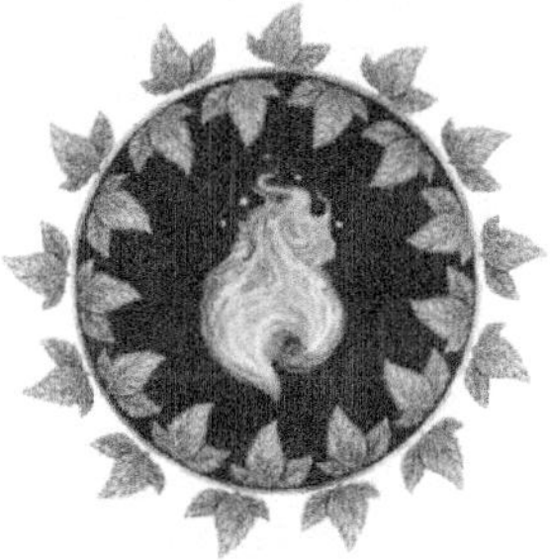
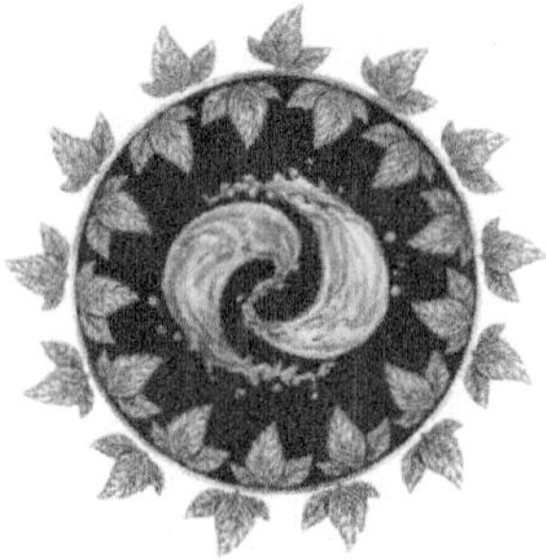

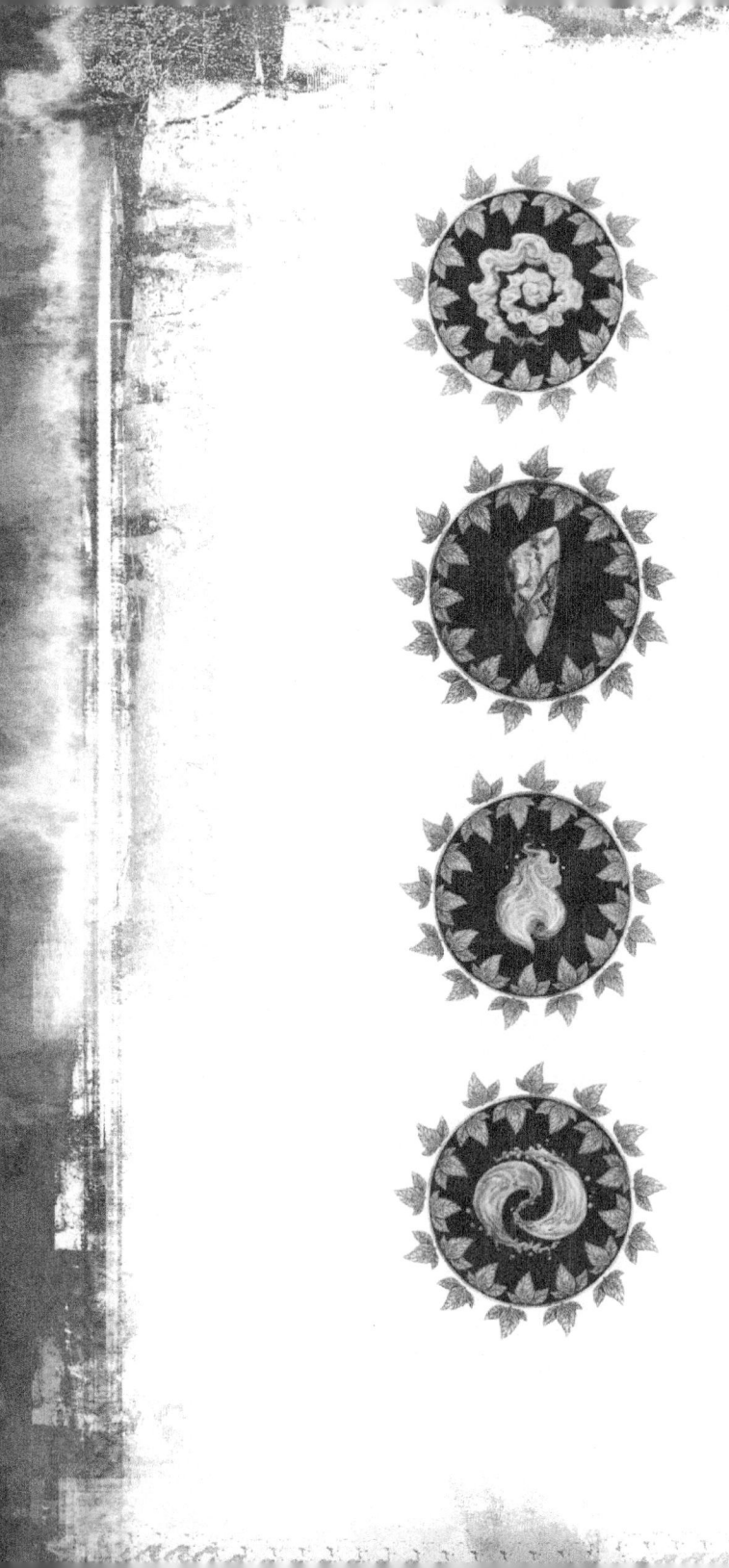

Chapter Twenty-Six

SARRS

The blood flows from her arm down my throat, refueling my magic reserves after the attack on the temple. I rip her arm out with my mouth and watch as her limp body falls into the pile that has gathered at my feet. Looking around, I see my advisors waiting for my orders.

"The four kings have betrayed me. I want their heads and I want the queen back here at my side." I growl.

"Of course, Sire." Gawain is hesitant, the idiotic fool.

"Don't test me, Gawain. I will gladly drain you of all your blood." He bows his head before speaking.

"We do not have a location on the five of them yet. The last they were seen was at the temple."

"It's been two fucking weeks, where would they be able to go? Get my most powerful mages in here now!" I scream. I know the only one

QUEEN OF KINGS

powerful enough to hide them all is Xander. They will all learn the consequences of their actions. Taking my red-headed pet. Making her whore herself out to them. Bile rises in my throat just thinking about it.

"Rialynne Faith is mine and I want her back. No matter what. Kill everyone in your path if you have to, just bring her here."

"Yes Sire." He bows and exits. I kick the pile of bodies before walking up to my king's guard.

"Get my throne room cleaned up." He bows before following my orders. They all fear me, which makes them respect me. I am not a fool, thinking that I earned it through loyalty and devotion. That is what they gave to Roderick and his whore of a wife. I want them to fear me.

I make my way out of the throne hall, down the corridor and straight to the door that leads down to the dungeons. Once I hit the stone floors, I cover my nose, trying to ward off the deadly smell coming from the area. A scream pierces through the air, making me smile as I enter the torture room.

"Are the ladies ready to talk?" I ask Marcus, my most skilled assassin and torturer.

"Sadly, they still seem intent on dying with their lips sealed." He responds and I look upon Rialynne's three ladies, Periwinkle, Stephanie, and Willow.

"We will not betray our queen." Willow says before spitting out her blood.

"Ares will burn you for your sins." Periwinkle snarls. I look at them and smile at their bravery. Few people would dare to speak to me in that manner.

"Ares cannot touch me. She has not come to save you, which means she does not exist." I tell them, making them gasp.

"Blasphemy!" Periwinkle shudders, making her chains rattle.

"No, fact. Now, tell me where Rialynne is, and I might grant you a swift death." They remain quiet, averting their eyes. I notice lady Stephanie has remained quiet. Her eyes seem glossed over, telling me she is either close to breaking, or death is calling her. I cannot have that. Approaching the bench, I pick up the iron needled, heating it with my fire magic until it sizzles red. I press it into her skin, but she does not flinch nor screams. It angers me. I can see her chest moving up and down, so I know she is not dead. "What's wrong with this one?"

"Nothing seems to work on her. She has no nerve endings. Or just an extremely high pain threshold." Marcus answers with a shrug.

I grip the lady's chin, but her eyes remain unmoving. I push off her and move onto Lady Willow. "Speak or I kill them both."

"Never." She spit. I wipe the spit from my face before pressing the searing metal to her stomach. She bares her teeth before letting out an ear-piercing scream.

"Good, you can feel pain, which means you will break. Tell me where she is." I yell, allowing my anger to consume me as I continue my assault on her body. She is panting and bleeding by the time I am done. "Speak. End your suffering. Death awaits you. Leave us with your honor intact."

"Dying for my queen is more honorable than betraying her." Willow answers through spaced out breaths. "I pray Ares will not show you any mercy when you meet her."

"So be it." Pushing more fire magic into the iron, I stab her in the chest, relishing in the pained scream from Periwinkle. I see a tear leave Stephanie out of the corner of my eye. Not so unbreakable. I leave the iron bar in Willow while going over and smacking Periwinkle. "Shut the fuck up or you're next. Tell me where she is."

"Burn in hell." She growls. I form a fireball in my hand, holding her mouth open as I force the fire down her throat. Killing her in the most painful way I believe someone could die. As her soul leaves her body I move onto Stephanie.

I caress her cheek before pressing a kiss to her lips. "This is your chance, my sweet lady. Learn from them and prove your loyalty to me."

"I... can't." She whispers and I smirk. I press another kiss to her and feel her kiss me back. Now I have her.

"Do you like it when I kiss you?" I ask her and she nods, ever so slightly. "Would you like me to kiss you again?"

"Yes."

I smirk.

"Tell me something useful and I will show you pleasure that can only be given to you by a king."

"There is a tracking device in her headband. Master Runk inserted it in case someone ever took her."

"Good girl. Tell me how I can track it." She doesn't speak and this time when I kiss her I deepen it by sticking my tongue down her throat. A moan erupts in her throat. I pull back and wait for her answer.

"A spell. It requires a spell." I wait for her to elaborate. "I am the only one who can perform it. I am a mage, and it requires certain things."

"I am assuming there's something you want in return for this? If I give you your freedom, will you perform the spell to bring my Rialynne back to me?" she nods. "What would you ask of me?"

"I don't want to die a virgin." She admits with a heated gaze. I brush her cheek.

"If I give you my cock, will you perform the spell and bring her to me?" She nods.

"I vow on pain of death."

"Yes, death will become you if you fail me. Very well, we have a deal." I find Marcus smirking at me before he removes Stephanie from the hanging chains. I catch her weak body, keeping up with our little game. I need her to find Rialynne.

"Get her cleaned up and prepare her for bed. Have her waiting for me in my quarters." Marcus nods, picking her up and exiting the room. "I'm coming for you, pet. Then I will not only have your crown, but your body will carry my heir."

"My king." Stephanie moans as I plunge my cock into her tight cunt. I have not had a virgin in a while, and I forgot how fucking good that feels. Her wrists and ankles are bound to the bedpost. I do not want her hands on me. I fuck her fast, pulling out spurting my seed all over her.

Getting up, I walk over and drink some water before pulling on a robe and leaving her. "Sire, is she ready?" Marcus asks.

"I gave her what she wanted. Get her out of my fucking room and performing that spell. I am going to wash. By the time I come back to the throne hall I expect her to have found my little red-headed pet." He smirks and bows.

Once I am showered and changed, I make my way back to the throne hall and notice Stephanie, Marcus, and Gawain all standing in a circle with something between them.

"My king." They all say with a bow.

"Well?" I ask, not to bother to elaborate.

"Lady Stephanie has not only figured out where they are, but also has found an interesting spell that could be useful to you." Marcus says with a smirk.

"Tell me." I say before taking a seat on my throne.

"There is a curse that will act like a restart." I raise my brow, not sure what she is instituting. "If you perform this curse, you can manipulate what everyone in the realm remembers. Alter their realities in whatever way you wish."

"Explain." I demand.

"For example, Rialynne thinks you are a bad person and the four kings are good. You could alter her to believe you are the good guy, and the kings are the evil ones." I rub my chin and a smile forms.

"What are the consequences of using this magic?" I ask, trying to prepare myself.

"It can be broken, but only by an act of true love." She speaks. "Seeing as that only happens between fated mates, it doesn't seem likely Rialynne would find hers."

"And if she does? Then what? All her memories return?"

"Everyone affected by the spell would remember everything. By then I thought it would be too late, because she would be your queen." She replied.

"Right. Very well. I would like to enact this curse immediately."

"Sire, we need all five of them in the same room at one time or else it won't work." I nod.

"Bring them here and perform it." She nods, and I cannot help but smile, because I am going to win. There is no one that will ever come between me and my rightful place upon the throne of Zavinia.

Hours pass and I begin to wonder if I should have gone with them to ensure the job is done correctly. A portal of magic opens, and eight bodies push through. Five are bound and bloodied.

"Get the fuck off me." Rialynne growls.

"Such a foul mouth you have." Her eyes find mine and where I expected to find fear, I see only hate and anger. "Not so powerful, are you?

And here I thought druids are supposed to be the best of the best."

"Your bitch used something to suppress our powers." She growls, and I look to Stephanie for an explanation.

"Just another spell. It's temporary but it should last long enough." Stephanie says.

"Long enough for what?" Xander asks. "You'll see." I smile.

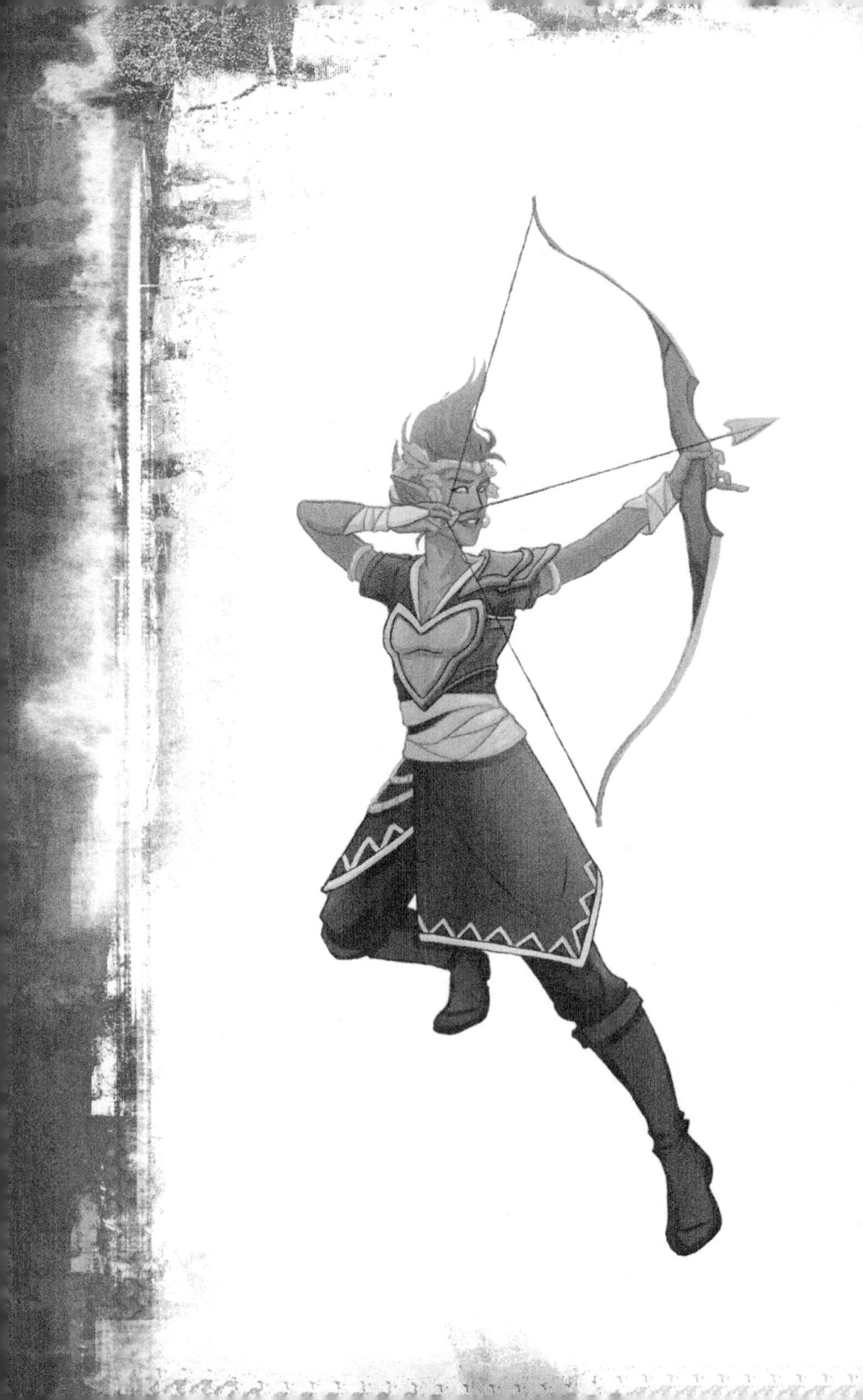

Chapter Twenty-Seven

RIALYNNE

I awake in Xander's arms and find him smiling at me, his thumb stroking the symbol that formed on my wrists when our mate bond snapped in place.

"Good morning." He smiles

"Morning." I kiss his nose. He flips me on my back with a claiming kiss. I open my legs to him, feeling his erection pressing against me. "Xander," I moaned, and he thrust into me.

"Yes, my mate?" He moves faster, and I dig my heels into his rear, urging him to go harder.

His hand moved between us, his finger circling my clit.

"Please." He pinches it and I clench down as my climax hits me. He muffles my scream with a kiss.

"Fuck, I could watch you do that all day." He growls and I flip us so I can ride him. Two hands come from behind me, and the scent of air and snow wash over me.

"Jett." I moan as I feel him pressing behind me.

"Do you want me too, Red?" He growls. "I could smell your arousal from all the way down in my room."

"Yes." I expected Xander to growl in protest, but he encourages Jett by pulling me down over him. I feel something wet coat my other hole before I feel Jett's tip presses into me. I wince and then moan with the pleasure that the pain brings.

"So, fucking perfect." Jett growls and I turn and kiss him. They begin to move, slowly first, allowing me to adjust, before picking up the pace. "Cum for us, Red." Jett commands, pinching my nipples before moving to my clit, adding pressure. I feel how close I am.

"Bite me, both of you." Without protest I feel them both pierce my flesh sending me over the edge. Xander on my breasts and Jett at my neck. I clench down screaming both their names as I climax. They follow soon after, unable to hold off. We slump down in a pile of tangled limbs.

"Good morning, Red." Jett smiles from behind me. I turn on my back to face him and smile.

"Good morning, Jett." I feel Xander wrap his arms around me. "There is something that I need to show you and the others."

"Yeah?" Jett asks. I feel Xander squeeze me in approval.

"Together." He kisses me and we get to our feet, finding discarded clothes and pulling them on before heading down the stairs that lead to the second level. Kai and Enzo are on the couch drinking coffee and smile once they see me.

"Good morning, Ria." They say at the same time as I descend the stairs. Each of them kisses me before we all sit down.

"So, last night something happened between me and Xander." I speak.

"I expected once I found you both naked and fucking." Jett smugly says.

Instead of saying anything, I just raise my marked wrists and wait for them to start freaking out.

"Your mate's bond snapped in place." Kai softly says.

"Yeah, but that doesn't mean I don't want you. I still want and need you all. I know it may seem impossible, but my soul still calls for you three as well." I say and watch as the three of them keep their faces blank.

"Please say something."

"Congrats, Red." Jett sounds defeated. Enzo looks like he might kill something, and Kai. Kai looks like he might just break.

"Guys…" I do not get to finish my sentence as the roof is blown to pieces. My body is knocked to the ground by Jett as he covers me. "What the fuck?"

"We're under attack." Jett growls, helping me to my feet.

"By whom? How did we get found?" I say looking for the others and seeing them all on their feet. We form a circle, our backs to each other with balls of our elements in our hands ready to strike.

"Hello, Rialynne." I look and see someone I never thought I would ever see. "Lady Stephanie, what are you doing?" I ask her. She smirks a menacing smirk and I notice she is no longer in her Cathedral uniform. Instead, is dressed in an all-black dress, showing off her beautiful body.

"My king needs his pet to return. I came to catch you and deliver you."

"No." All four kings growl at once forming a protective circle around me.

"You'll have to get through us." Xander growls.

"You're not taking my mate."

My heart thunders at his proclamation and Stephanie smiles.

"You won't have a choice." Magic unlike any I have ever seen before erupts from her and knocks us all onto our asses. My magic locks up inside me. I try to call on it, but nothing comes forth.

"What did you do?" I try to stand. My body fails me.

"Just a little spell I learned from my days as an apprentice. Don't worry, your magic will return but not for a while, and by then it will be too late." Her long black nails grip my chin and look into my eyes.

"Why?" I croak.

"Listen to me," she whispered. I am confused until I see two guards taking my kings into custody. "I would never betray you Ria, but you need to listen to me. You will not remember any of this but just know that I am doing it to save you. Trust in your heart and follow it."

"What do you mean?" Tears escape as she binds my hands. She picks me up and whispers in my ear.

"Follow your heart back to them. Then the curse will be broken." She whispers before we are pushed through a portal.

"Get the fuck off me." I growl.

"Such a foul mouth you have." My eyes find the owner of that voice and I let him see all the hate and anger I have for him. "Not so powerful, are you? And here I thought druids are supposed to be the best of the best."

"Your bitch used something to suppress our powers." I growl, and watch as he looks towards Stephanie for an explanation.

"Just another spell. It's temporary but it will last long enough." Stephanie says.

"Long enough for what?" Xander asks.

"You'll see." He smiles, and my gut wrenches.

"Perform the curse." I hear Sarrs say, and I realize this must be what Stephanie meant. "Wait." I plead and Sarrs holds her off. "Please let me say good-bye to them."

"You really are a whore, aren't you? How disappointing you have become. Spread your legs for them. Why should I allow this?" Sarrs says.

"Because it will not matter, will it? Once she performs whatever spell next, I will be yours. At least grant me this one request." I plead, and look at my kings who all have deadly glares in their eyes. Sarrs lift me to my feet, and my bindings are cut free. His hands cup my face and I try not to grimace at his touch.

I watch as his eyes wander down my body. I try to hide my new mark, but I fail. He pulls it up and snarls at me. "You've bonded with the mage. I can't have that." He growls.

"There's nothing you can do about it." Xander growls, and Sarrs smirks. I try to wrench my hand free, but my body is so weak.

"Don't, please." I beg him as the tears begin to pour, but it's too late. He wraps a hand around my wrists and proceeds to burn my skin, making a blood-curdling scream erupt my throat. I hear Xander scream and charge for Sarrs, but he is knocked back with air magic. "Doesn't matter, Ria. You're still my mate." Xander yells as I slump to the floor, cradling my burned arm.

"Get up, Red." Jett growls, hurt lacing his throat.

"Ria." Enzo reaches for me, and I crawl to him.

"This is the queen you want. Look at how pathetic she is." A boot kicks into my ribs, and I feel blood pooling in my mouth.

"I'm going to fucking kill you." All four kings growl, in some manner.

I am ripped from the floor by my hair. "No, you won't. Because you will forget you ever met her, just as she won't remember you." He smirks, and a cloud of dark magic consumes the entire throne hall.

My eyes fall close, and I allow myself to drift into the abyss. Xander's voice calling my name is the last thing I hear as I lose myself completely. My entire life was taken from me in the blink of an eye. The family that I had come to find and love, ripped from me. Everything that I ever shared with them fades away. Disappearing. All the times we laughed. All the love we confessed to one another. All the memories of my life erased, leaving a hole inside my soul.

My heart bleeds as I cry until I don't know why I am crying anymore.

Looking around, I find myself in my bed with the book I was reading clutched in my hand. A dark romance book about kings and queens.

Something that can only be found in fairytales. I look at my phone and notice it's well past midnight. I close the book, allowing myself to drift off to dreamland again. Tomorrow is a new day.

The alarm to my phone rings loudly as I reach over and turn it off. Looking down, I see that I fell asleep in my jeans and t-shirt again. Looking at the clock it reads 5:30 A.M. Groaning, I throw the covers off me before getting up and changing into my running clothes.

"Good morning, Little Red." Dad says from the kitchen as I grab a bottle of water from the fridge. "First day of school, are you ready?"

"Of course. It's college. Don't tell me you're going to be all sappy?" I ask, turning just in time to catch the apple he has thrown at me.

"Nope, just don't forget to come home every once in a while."

"I will. See you later." I exit out the front door and start running down the trail that maps out the five-mile circle of Klestria. I pass by the Cathedral and something familiar washes over me, but I shrug it off. I have never been inside there, nor do I have any desire to.

I make it back to the house, shower, and change into my school uniform before lugging my suitcase out and summoning a portal. Stepping out the other side, I smile at the iron-clad gate that leads into Klestria Academy. My home for the next four years.

"Welcome to the academy, Miss Faith." I smile at the Dean as he hands me the handbook. "I hope you succeed in all your classes and do not forget if you are interested in trying out for your house's team, tryouts will be on Wednesday from 6:00 P.M. to 8:00 P.M."

"Thank you, Sir." I smile and then eye his name plaque. "Is Ziba a family name?" He smiles at me, placing his coffee mug down.

"Yes, my father's."

"I should get going." He nods and I make my way out of the office.

"Don't forget, Miss Faith," I turn and see him smiling at me. "I will be watching you."

A shiver runs down my spine and the hairs raise at the back of my neck.

"Creep." I mutter to myself.

"Welcome to Klestria Academy. All first years need to head to Training North for the induction ceremony." An announcement starts. A tall water elemental human with mahogany brown hair is controlling the flow of student traffic, and I follow it.

I find all the other fire elementals and take my seat. The noise quiets down as Dean Ziba steps into the middle of the platform. A scent of fire and ash runs over me, and that sense of familiarity hits me again. I find my gaze locked onto a fire rogue with shaggy brown hair and rounded human ears. Something inside me recognizes him, but the feeling leaves just as fast as it came. I look back towards the Dean just as he begins his welcoming speech.

"Welcome to Klestria Academy! It's going to be a momentous year."

Epilogue

With a curse looming over the world of Zavinia, the patrons have no memory of their past lives. The beloved four kings and queens are trapped in a reality where they do not know who they are or the fate that bonds them to each other. As Rialynne begins her first year at Klestria Academy, new friends and enemies threaten her position at the school.

The four kings are adopted by two blood elves. Their parents were killed as a result of something Rialynne Faith's mother did, or so they are told. Sarr's Bane seeks her power, using the four of them to manipulate her and bring her to him.

What will be in store for our five royals? Will they begin to remember their past as their new reality brings them closer together?

AUTHOR NOTE

Thank you so much for reading my first reverse harem. I hope the cliffhanger did not hit too hard, but I worked so hard to try and figure out how I wanted to introduce Zavinia and the cast of characters.

Do not worry, I will not leave you waiting too long in between books. If you enjoyed it, please kindly leave a review on Goodreads/Amazon/Barnes & Noble, and any social media platform of your choosing.

If you are interested in discussing this book, you can join my reading group on Facebook: https://www.facebook.com/groups/1079372232891537/

ACKNOWLEDGMENTS

First and foremost, I would like to continually thank my wonderful family for continuing to support my journey. Even the times they joke about the smut that I love to write. I will always thank my husband for encouraging me to keep writing no matter what imposter syndrome is saying.

To my readers, especially Vivi who continues to give me her honest feedback every time I run her past an idea I have. The time she dedicates to me as a critique partner helps me so much. Her love for my crazy mood and plot changes keeps me going.

To my parents, especially my two Mothers that love to read everything I write and buy my books no matter what it is about. I appreciate you both and love you with all my heart.

ABOUT THE AUTHOR

C.M. Hano is a small-town author from Southeast Georgia. Her love for Adult Fantasy inspires her to continue to create magical worlds readers can escape to. She is best known for her Dark Fantasy Romance Title *Blood Oath: A Princess Chronicles Novel* and LGBTQ Fantasy TarotVerse series. She lives a charming life with her husband and two daughters.

STAY IN TOUCH

- : C. M. Hano
- : @HanoCera
- : @cerahano
- : @cmhano_author

Reading Group: C. M. Hano's Reading Warriors

ALSO BY C.M HANO
The Princess Chronicles series

The Orion Novellas
The Journey Begins
The Hollow Realm
The War back Home

Blood & Shadow
Blood Oath
Shadow Light

PNR Standalone
Night & Day

TarotVerse
Xora
Whitfrost

The Cursed Parlay Series
The Cursed Parlay
Across The Starless Sky

Printed in Great Britain
by Amazon